FRAMED IN GUILT

Dane rode into El Amaro to find a man — a man who had caused him to be outlawed and branded as a ruthless killer. But he soon discovered that he had ridden into the middle of a range war, and in the wild confusion he heard enough to convince him that the man he sought was the sheriff's son. It was common talk that he was riding with a pack of gun-wolves intent on terrorizing cattlemen and freighters alike. Dane was hunted by both the sheriff and the outlaws, but he refused to back down. It was a case of win or die.

LESTER DAVIDSTON

◆

FRAMED IN GUILT

Complete and Unabridged

LINFORD
Leicester

First hardcover edition published in Great Britain
in 2002 by Robert Hale Limited, London

Originally published in paperback as
The Lone Gun by Chuck Adams

First Linford Edition
published 2004
by arrangement with
Robert Hale Limited, London

British Library CIP Data

Davidston, Lester, *1928* –
    Framed in guilt.—Large print ed.—
Linford western library
1. Western stories
2. Large type books
I. Title II. Adams, Chuck, *1919* –. Lone gun
823.9′14 [F]

ISBN 1–84395–261–0

Published by
F. A. Thorpe (Publishing)
Anstey, Leicestershire

Set by Words & Graphics Ltd.
Anstey, Leicestershire
Printed and bound in Great Britain by
T. J. International Ltd., Padstow, Cornwall
This book is printed on acid-free paper

1

Jasper Trail

It was a wide world of deep blue sky, green grass growing in patches, and in the near distance, multi-hued rock, that confronted Dane Averill as he turned his mount off the high, mountain trail and into the valley that stretched out in front of him in the early heat of the afternoon. Little curved hills wandered down and down into the purple-hazed mountains that marched off on the skyline and behind him, other tall crests along whose trails he had ridden for the past seven days, brooded high against the sunlit heavens. Harsh and unyielding as the hills had been, this valley was a world of scented breezes and softer, soothing sounds which were like a balm to his tired body.

He reined his mount on a long,

grassy promontory, letting the animal blow, his grey eyes speculative as he turned his head slowly to survey the vast sweep of the Blackwater range that rolled away in the distance. Sitting back in the saddle, resting his body with a rider's ease, he up-tilted his wide-brimmed hat and dug in his pockets for the makings of a smoke. The heat had been bad during the morning as he had made his way down the scarred side of the hills and he had needed to find this valley for water. Up there, the streams were nothing more than dried out channels in the rocks and dirt. Here and there, he had come across a patch of semi-solid mud which had not yet dried out in the harsh sunlight. Drought had come to this part of the territory, but here in the valley, there was a greenness which promised water for himself and grass for his mount.

Even as he smoked, drawing the pleasant-smelling smoke into his lungs, Dane was alert. Twice during the night he had been wakened by the sound of

2

riders in the hills, vague echoes as they rode along other trails than that on which he had found himself. Finishing his smoke, he dug deeper in his pocket, came up with the carefully folded piece of paper. It looked as if it had been creased and thumbed many times. There was a smear of dirt on the back of it as he unfolded it slowly and stared down at it, his face hard, expressionless. Just an ordinary piece of paper. There were literally hundreds of them scattered all over this part of the state; some nailed to trees, others nesting in the drawers or on the walls of a score of sheriff's offices. A wanted poster, offering five thousand dollars reward for the capture of the man whose picture appeared on it, five thousand dollars for this man, dead or alive.

What made it so interesting for him, was that the face which stared back at him from the poster was his own!

He sat quite still for several moments, then folded the poster with an equal care and replaced it in his pocket. He had carried it for more than half a year now, since that day when he had been falsely branded as an outlaw and killer by the man he had known only as Chico. The other had not been a Mexican, and it had been pretty clear to him that this had not been his real name. But whatever his name was, wherever he happened to be, Dane meant to track him down and kill him.

Wheeling his mount, he moved down off the promontory towards the lower ground. He heeled the bay slowly around in a wide circle, listening for any sudden sound, but he had travelled for several minutes before he heard anything out of the ordinary; then he came suddenly alert as he saw something move down on the flats at the foot of the valley, several miles away. Putting his mount into the lee of a low rise, he watched the indistinct form which drifted from the rocks and patches of hollow bush down below, heading over the rough country that lay ahead of him, urging his mount forward at a

4

punishing pace, covering ground speedily. The reason for his hurry was soon apparent. More men emerged from the tangled brush country; Dane estimated almost ten or a dozen of them. Now they had their quarry in the open, they began to spread out behind the fleeing man, the outermost men riding faster than the others so that they curved around in a wide semi-circle, the horns beginning to close in on the foremost rider.

Frowning a little, Dane edged his mount forward. That rider down there sure looked as if he was in trouble, mighty big trouble; and those odds were ones than Dane didn't like. Guiding his mount off the narrow, winding trail, he plunged through a stretch of grassland, then over rough, stony ground that slowed him considerably. Not until he reached level ground at the foot of the hills was he able to push his mount. He could hear nothing of the riders now, guessed they had caught their quarry and were probably deciding what to do with him. If he knew the kind of man they bred out here, the hunted man would be given short thrift and they would string him up with a riata from the nearest convenient tree.

Brush abounded in tall clumps here but there was plenty of evidence that the riders had ridden through here a little while earlier. He moved on, cutting between tall, upthrusting boulders, moving across the valley floor at an angle, heading in the direction where he reckoned the hunted man would have been caught if that closing circle of men had caught up with him. The burning weight of the afternoon sun lay on his back and shoulders and he eased the Colts in their worn holsters absently, touching the metal with his long fingers. Some five minutes later, he came upon a long slide of loose shale that stretched across his path. A quick glance told him that the others had come this way. There was a new slide in the dirt a little to his right where they had put their horses to the slope and without hesitation, he did likewise. The bay fought for footing as it slid down the slope, dust rising around its haunches. It reached the bottom of the slide in a cloud of dust and fine gravel. Rounding a huge boulder which almost blocked the trail at this point, he came on to a flat bench of land, perhaps a quarter of a mile long, and headed across it at speed, touching the flanks of his mount with the rowels. It responded gallantly and on the other side of the bench, although there was no sign of the horsemen, he spotted more tracks in the softer earth, knew now that they could not be far away. Directly in front of him was a stretch of timber, first-year growth pine, stretching up high into the heavens. There was a warning tremor in his body now, but he thrust it away as he put his mount into the trees.

He was fifty yards in when he picked out the sudden yell. It seemed to come from his right and he wheeled his mount instantly, heading towards it.

The echo of the shout died away and there was an oppressive silence among the trees now. But he knew that he had not been mistaken.

A few moments later, there was the sharp snicker of a horse. Dane gigged his mount forward and came out into the circular clearing a few seconds later. The men he had seen earlier wore clustered in a tight group around the short, red-faced man they had been pursuing. The scene was a grim, but common one. Dane took in everything in one rapid sweep of the grey eyes and it didn't need any stretch of the imagination to tell what was about to happen here.

The short man had been seated on his horse again, under the long, outstretching branch of the towering tree. His shirt had been torn and there was a smear of blood down one cheek and another across his bare chest. The film of sweat on his face was clearly visible in the soft light that filtered down into the clearing.

Dane's glance flickered briefly in the direction of the sharp-featured man who seemed to be the leader of this group, the man who sat his saddle, the coiled rope held loosely between his fingers. The measure of their concentration was evident in the fact that none of them seemed to have heard his approach, although it had been impossible to move quietly through the twig-crackling underbrush.

The man seated beneath the branch saw him first and a look of hope flashed across his sweat-glistening features. His hands had been tied behind his back and he sat the saddle with difficulty, unable to control the bucking mount.

The men turned suddenly, then sat frozen in surprise. A look of hostility came into their gazes, then the oldest man, the hatchet-faced individual, moved out of the ring a little way, still holding the riata, said slowly: 'Seems to me like yuh've stumbled on somethin' that don't concern yuh, mister. Reckon it'd be better if yuh was to ride on and ferget this.'

There was a hard, challenging smile on Dane's lips. 'Guess I'm just bein' curious, but these seem pretty long odds to me. Ten men against one.'

A tall, broad-shouldered man edged his way forward, placed his mount alongside the oldster's. 'Guess yuh didn't hear what Mr Skinner said, stranger.' There was a note of glacial menace in his thin voice. 'Yuh're askin' fer trouble if yuh don't ride along like he says.'

Dane turned his attention to the man who spoke, let his gaze rest on him for a moment. He nodded almost casually. 'What's he done? Rustler, murderer?'

'Ain't none o' yore business.'

'I reckon, in the circumstances, I might be makin' it my business.' His glance flicked to the man on the horse, still perspiring freely, although there was a fresh look of hope now in his eyes, as if he saw this stranger as a deliverer, come at the last minute to save him from the inevitable rope. 'You killed somebody, mister? Taken some o' their cattle?'

'I ain't taken none o' their beef.' The other coughed, tried to wipe his mouth on the side of his shirt where it hung in tatters around his shoulders.

The broad-shouldered man made to say something more, but it was the sharp-featured Skinner who spoke up. 'I'll do the talkin' Matson,' he snapped. His gimlet eyes rested on Dane. 'Yuh figgerin' on takin' on the lot of us, getting yoreself killed just because o' this tinhorn thief?' His hard gaze was dangerous. 'Reckon yore hearin' can't be as good as it should be in these parts. Yuh poke yore nose into my affairs and by God, yuh're sure as good as dead.'

There was no doubting the threat in Skinner's harsh voice, yet the words seemed to have no effect at all on the man who sat easily in the saddle, facing him and the rest of his men. Then Dane gave a crooked grin. 'This looks more'n more like a necktie party that's been

11

arranged for some time. What have they got on you, Mister?'

'Nothin'.' declared the other sharply, his voice still tinged with fear. 'They just want me out of the way so they can go on with their murderin' — ' He stopped short as one of the men nearest him suddenly lashed out with a tightly bunched fist, catching him full in the mouth. The man reeled in his saddle, almost fell being unable to help himself, but somehow managed to retain his balance.

The muscles of Dane's jaw lumped under the skin. One of the men uttered a harsh laugh, said thinly: 'I say string him up, Skinner; and if this *hombre* cares, he can join him at the end of another rope.'

'You talk too big, mister,' said Dane thinly. His gaze locked with that of the man who had struck the other. 'I'll remember your face and when I next meet you, believe me, you'll live to regret it.'

For a moment, there was stark

disbelief on the faces of the men in the group. Then Skinner said tautly: 'Yuh've been warned, *hombre*. We don't like folk hornin' in on anythin' we do in these parts.' His threat had merely been a feint to cover what he really intended to do. Without warning, his right hand struck downward for the gun at his belt. It moved in a blur of speed, but Dane had anticipated him, had guessed the kind of gunslingers these were who would hunt down an unarmed man and try to string him from the nearest tree without a trial of any kind.

Before any man there rightly knew what was happening, they found themselves staring down the death-dealing ends of a pair of long-barrelled Colts, balanced easily and stone steady in the stranger's hands. Three of the men had started to draw with Skinner. Now they let the half-drawn guns slide back into their holsters. No point in taking chances with a man as fast as this, although for a brief second, the possibility lived in their eyes. The hard look on the stranger's face told them quite clearly that one false move would bring them nothing but a slug in the heart.

'Yuh're makin' a big mistake, mister,' snarled Skinner, his hand resting on the butt of his gun. Then he moved it slowly and deliberately until it had strayed to the pommel of his saddle.

'Mebbe so.' Dane's tone was flat. 'If this *hombre* is a rustler like you say, then I ain't goin' to stand in your way. But it seems to me that every man has the right to be heard by an unbiased jury, and I reckon there ain't a man among you could be called unbiased.'

'Mister,' called the short, balding man on the horse, 'these men want me out of this valley so they can move in and take over.'

Silence held for a second. Dane said: 'They got any reason for that?'

'They don't need no reason to run a man out of the territory. If he won't run then they kill him.'

Dane nodded. Somehow, he believed

this man. The other looked more like a sodbuster than a rustler. He doubted if the little man knew how to handle a gun. 'I figure you'd better ride on out of here while the goin's good. Get movin'.'

The other looked wildly about him for a moment as if expecting one of the watching, waiting men to stop him, then he kneed his mount, urged it forward through the clustered ring of men until he drew level with Dane. 'Thanks, mister,' he said tightly. 'I ain't goin' to forget this in a hurry.'

'Never mind about the thanks,' snapped Dane harshly, not once taking his glance off the men in front of him, knowing that they only wanted him to relax his vigilance for a split second and they would nail him. 'Just get out of here. Next time, take more care to have some of your own kind around you when coyotes like these pay you a call.'

'Sure, sure.' The other nodded quickly. His adam's apple bobbed up and down nervously as he swallowed.

Then he somehow succeeded in wheeling his mount with his knees and set it moving through the thick brush. Dane settled down in the saddle. His gaze flickered from one man to another, watching the faces, eyeing them all closely and carefully so that he would know each one of them again. For one moment, when he had first spotted them, he had hoped that the man he was trailing might be among them. This was the sort of thing the other would relish. But he was not there.

There was a glitter of sardonic amusement in Skinner's eyes as he sat with his hands on the saddle horn. He seemed to have regained a lot of his lost confidence.

'Yore time is runnin' mighty short, mister,' he said thinly. 'We can always lay our hands on Maller again whenever we've a mind to. But yuh ain't goin' to live long even if yuh manage to get away from here — which ain't likely.'

'Don't fret none about me,' grunted

Dane. 'Whoever dies, you'll go first, Skinner.'

'Yuh aimin' to use that gun?' grunted Skinner. He shook his head slowly, not once shifting his gaze. 'I don't think you really will.'

As the other spoke, two of his men went for their guns. Fast men with a gun, deadly fast. But even as their weapons lifted into line, the twin Colts spoke death. Thunder filled the small clearing as the two guns blazed as one. The short, round-faced man went down, sliding from the saddle, clutching at his chest. The other man reared up as if trying to stand on tiptoe in the saddle. He screamed wildly as he dropped the gun and lifted both bands to his face, then nodded like a drunken man before he slipped into a still thing on the ground under the feet of his mount.

The horses reared and bucked and men fought to keep themselves in the saddle, striving to hold the mounts in, clearly wanting to draw on him but having no desire to go the same way as their two companions.

Skinner stared up at Dane, his neck muscles corded like string under the flesh, his eyes bleak and filled with the promise of death. In the distance, as the last of the echos died away, Dane picked out the faint sound of a horse crashing through the brush. Another few minutes and the man he had saved from a rope would be away to safety.

Before the bucking horses could be fully brought under control, Dane suddenly whipped his own mount around and raced it off into the brush, bending low in the saddle. He expected a hail of lead to follow him across the clearing before he could make the safety of the trees, but as he had hoped, his sudden move had taken the men by surprise. Branches whipped across his face as he straightened a little in the saddle, thrusting the guns back into their holsters, then reaching for the reins to guide the plunging mount along the narrow, twisting path that led

18

in the same direction as that taken by the nester. Behind him, there was a confused shouting as the men tried to urge their mounts to follow him. Vaguely, he was aware of Skinner roaring orders at the top of his lungs. Then the trees and bushes had closed in behind him and he was running for the rocks on the far side of the belt of trees. Every second he was sure a rifle would bark from the timber at his back and a bullet would find its mark. But the others seemed to be taking their time riding through the trees and he had covered the open stretch of ground before the first of them came into sight.

Down the long dip he rode, nursing his mount. At the bottom they splashed through a shallow stream, then up a stony bank and into more thickets which grew shoulder high here, dense clumps of mesquite and thorn that ripped at his arms and legs, raking with long, thorny fingers along his flesh. With another look over the empty ground at the back of him, he rode on through the thorn, then up a wide, grassy slope and it was here that he came up with the man he had saved.

Somehow, the other had managed to loosen the bonds around his wrists and was rubbing them with his fingers where the cords had burned ugly-red welts into his flesh. The man was still red in the face and perspiring profusely. He gave the ground immediately behind them an apprehensive glance.

'You figure we've thrown 'em off, mister?'

'Could be. You know this part of the country well?'

'I guess I should. I own most of it.' The other's brow puckered. 'But you must be a stranger around here or you'd never have put in your nose when they tried to finish me back there. Ain't many men who'll go up against Ed Skinner alone — and nobody I know of who'd do it when he has his men there to back him up. I want to thank you for putting in your hand back there.'

He proferred his hand and Dane

grasped it, feeling the firm strength in the other's grip. The man's gaze was open and full of gratitude. 'You just ridin' through or lookin' for a job?'

'Riding or shooting?' queried the other with a faint smile.

The other's brows went up. 'A little of each,' he said frankly. 'Maybe more of one than the other.'

'Seems to me that you lead a pretty dangerous life in these parts. Those men were sure hell bent on destroying you. Why did they try to hang you back there?'

'Let's ride back to the spread first. We can talk there,' concluded the other abruptly. 'Besides, even though I don't see any of those polecats around here, I still don't feel too safe. A bullet can come out of any bush and without any warnin'.'

They swung north to higher ground and everything shimmered about them in the day's heat. Maller led the way along half-hidden trails and it was soon evident that he knew these hills better than most. There was a wide area of more mesquite and low cactus and then the ground grew more inviting as they rode along the smooth valley floor, keeping a sharp eye open on the hilly crests which lifted on either side of the trail. But Skinner and his men seemed to have called off their hunt for some reason known only to themselves and they saw nothing of the men. Climbing a low, undulating rise they came within sight of the creek that ran through the valley and beside it, the trim log house set in the tree-ringed hollow, within sight and sound of the creek. Dane saw a bunch of cattle on the far slope and more than a dozen horses in a pole corral built in front of the house. They reined their mounts in front of the long, low porch, with the slant roof dipping down to within five feet of the ground. Plenty of shade and coolness there, thought Dane, even in the heat of the high noon.

'Nice place you've got here,' he said as he slid from the saddle.

'Took me a long time to get all of this,' commented the other. 'Had to buy the land and build everything. There's an empire here, you know, and it's all mine. I've built it out of nothing with my bare hands.'

'Reckon I can understand how you feel about it.' Dane's brow creased. 'And those killers want to run you out of the territory.'

The other nodded. They stepped on to the porch and Maller said: 'I'll get some chow ready, Victoria — that's my daughter — is in town with the buggy. Won't be back much before evening.' He nodded towards the cupboard. 'You'll find whiskey in there if you'd like a drink to wash some of that trail dust out of your throat.'

He went through into the kitchen and Dane crossed over to the cupboard, took out one of the bottles and a couple of glasses, poured himself a generous drink and drank slowly, letting the raw liquor slide smoothly down his throat and into his empty stomach. Through the window, he scanned the herd of cattle on the nearby rise. Not a big herd, but then this man had the air of a nester about him. He was certainly no cattleman like those men who had tried to string him up. Why had they wanted to kill him in that way? Just to get rid of him? But it would have been quicker and simpler just to shoot him down, leave his body out there where the jackals could get it. This was cattle country and in any of the towns, the sheriffs were on the side of the cattlemen. The tag of rustler had only to be put to a man, especially a sodbuster, and every man's hand would be against him and it would be open season for shooting him down, or stringing him from a tree.

Maller came in, bringing plates of fried potatoes, beef straight from the pan and beans. Bread and hot coffee followed and Dane pulled a chair to the table and sat down as the other motioned him forward.

'Eat up,' said the other. 'Plenty more

where that came from if you're still hungry when you've finished.'

Dane's teeth gnawed at dry lips for a moment. He tasted the beef, nodded.

'It's all from my own herd,' said the other across the table. 'No rustled beef here. You can ride out over my spread and take a look see for yourself. I don't ship any beef out by the railroad. Just keep enough for my own use. I'm not a cattle man.'

'I guessed that when I first saw you,' grunted Dane. 'Besides, there's no reason why a bunch of cattlemen should try to string up another of their number. Men like that stick together.'

Maller hesitated. For a moment he looked distinctly uncomfortable. Then he nodded.

'You evidently don't belong in these parts,' he observed.

'That's right. I'm lookin' for a man.'

'Any particular man?' inquired the other, glancing up. There was a spark of interest in his eyes.

'Very particular,' Dane agreed. 'When

I find him, I mean to kill him.'

Maller shrugged. 'I guessed from the way you handled that gun; you might be that kind of man. You runnin' from the law?'

'Does that make any difference?'

'Not as far as I'm concerned,' asserted Maller. 'You saved my life back there and I ain't likely to forget that no matter what you've done.'

'The trouble is that I did nothin' except get on the wrong side of one man. He had me branded a killer and outlaw, set the law on my trail and I've been keepin' one jump ahead of 'em all the time.'

'You reckon this man might be in these parts?' asked the other suspiciously as he chewed thoughtfully on a mouthful of food.

At length, Dane's plate was empty and the cup drained by his side. The other poured out more coffee and Dane held it under his nose for a moment, savouring the fragrance. These were the things he had missed more than anything else on the trail.

'Excellent coffee,' he said appreciatively. The other had listened intently to what he had to say. 'You think these men may pay you another visit?'

'Hard to say. Wouldn't surprise me in the least.'

'You seem very unconcerned. Back there when I found you, you were scared to death.'

'Back there, I was off my own ground. Here, I have my own men, men who came with me from back east, men I can trust and who will watch every trail that leads into this valley. Skinner will need a bigger force of killers at his back to take me by surprise again and finish me.'

Dane stared at the other in surprise. There was no doubting that he meant every word he said. The man seemed to exude confidence now. A sudden gleam came into his eyes.

'Perhaps I could help you find this man you're lookin' for. Might repay you a little for savin' my life.'

Dane shrugged, rising to his feet. 'Thanks for the grub,' he said quietly; 'I needed that after bein' so long on the trail. As for the man I'm lookin' for, I reckon the place for me to start lookin' will be El Amaro.'

'You ridin' into town, just like that?' Maller lifted his brows into a tight line. 'You're a goshdarned fool if you do.'

'I'm used to trouble, if that's what you mean.'

'More'n trouble. You killed two of Skinner's men back there when you saved me and none of them *hombres* is likely to forget it. He'll have men watchin' the town for you. You won't be around long enough to think things over.'

At the door, Dane paused. 'These cattlemen who're trying to move you off the valley. Why don't you get all of the other nesters together, form some sort of force against 'em? It's goin' to be your only chance of survival. If you let things go much longer, they'll grind you into the ground.'

'Try to fight the cattlemen — and start a full-scale range war here?' Maller retorted with a harsh laugh. He shook his head swiftly. 'How long do you really think that would last, and more to the point, who do you reckon would win?'

'I get your point,' Dane nodded. There was no answer to that. The other was speaking horse sense. 'But when a man has to carry a load of vengeance like this, he has to do what he must.'

The other nodded grimly. 'If you should need help, you know where to come. I've got men here who'll ride with me.'

'I'll remember that,' Dane's mouth thinned into a tight line. He tightened the cinch under the bay's belly, saddled up and rode out of the hollow, up the wide ridge on which the herd of cattle grazed peacefully. There was little here to hint of the possibility of a range war. Several of the men, squatting in a small hollow on the side of the ridge around a blazing fire, eyed him curiously, but no one made any move to stop him and he guessed that the fact he had ridden in from the direction of the lodge exempted him from the chance of being an enemy.

Once over the lip of the rise, Dane rode with extreme caution, eyes alert. There was no way of telling which bush might hide an enemy and there was no knowing the lengths Ed Skinner might go to in order to keep him from butting further into his business. It was certain that he wanted the Maller place — but why? It would not make good cattle land. As far as he had been able to see, there was only that one broad stretch of real grassland on the lee of the hill, overlooking the ranch itself which was suitable for grazing a beef herd. So there had to be some other reason for wanting it, some reason he couldn't see at the moment.

He moved on through the hills, now in more of a hurry than he had been before. The thought of Maller disturbed him a little. Could be that the other was just a little too sure of himself. So far, whenever there had been any feud between the cattlemen and the nesters who were trying to move in and take over the range, trying to parcel it up into neat squares, edging it around with barbed wire, blocking the vast open spaces where only the buffalo and then the lean, long-horned cattle roamed, it had always been the nesters who had come off worst. They were not gunmen. They came out here from the east, taking the land which the Government in Washington had handed down to them. The cattlemen had held this country long before the settlers began to move in, and they meant to hold it by every means at their disposal, none of them would stop at gunplay to keep what they regarded as rightfully theirs, in spite of the land deeds which the Government gave to the nesters.

He had no liking for the sodbusters himself. In their presence here, he foresaw the end of the open ranges, foresaw the coming of men who would hammer this country into a network of railroads and stage lines, build their huge cities and fill the air with smoke and pollution. But if a man bought his land, then he had an inalienable right to do with it as he wished. That was why they had fought the war, why men had died.

He was well into the hills when he heard the staccato beat of riders behind him, coming up fast. Deliberately, he turned off the road into the thick brush, waited until the men went by. In the softer sunlight of late afternoon, he watched the men carefully. Even as he sat still and silent in the saddle, he realized that the dust lifted from the trail in his own wake would surely give him away, must warn these riders if they did not know already that he was riding ahead of them. But they rode by without slackening their pace, without looking to right or left and gradually, the hammer of their mounts faded into the distance along the trail, until finally, there was only a faintly diminishing murmur at the edge of his hearing. He had seen little of the faces of the men who had ridden by at such a fast pace, but he had noticed enough to realize that they had not been the men who had tried to string up Maller and he had caught a fragmentary glimpse of the silver star on the shirt of the man leading the group. A posse of some kind, he decided, as he urged his mount back on to the trail.

Sunlight made a trembling glow on the branches of the trees which overhung the trail. There was still a considerable warmth in the air, but most of the dust which had made riding a torture during the past few days, seemed to have settled out of the air which was clean and pure. A little later, he crossed another trail that twisted around the base of the hills and led off to the south west, intersecting the one on which he travelled. According to his reckoning, he was now less than five miles from El Amaro and knew he would reach it before dark. His mount frequently slowed, knowing its own mind and he made no effort to push it any further.

★ ★ ★

El Amaro stood on a bench of low ground, with the hills that Dane had seen earlier standing as a tall backcloth in the near distance. They were closer to the town than he had expected and two trails ran off into the lower foothills, disappearing into the purple dusk as he crossed a narrow, wooden bridge which spanned the broad, sluggish river and road into the main street of the town. The sun had dipped down below the western horizon shortly before he had reached the town, and the world was now a deep blue place, full of shadows, with the cool air of evening, flowing down off the mountains, a faint pressure on his face. In the town itself, there was even the smell of the hills in the air and the horse increased its gait a little as if sensing that they had at last come to the end of their journey.

A double row of buildings on either side of the road which ran straight on through El Amaro picked out the main part of town. There were other buildings in the distance, scattered through the waterblue dusk, several with yellow lights already gleaming behind the small, square windows. A typical cattle town, which had sprung up on the trail where the river formed a natural barrier and also an excellent meeting place for the huge herds driven down from the plains to the east and north.

He rode between the single-storey houses that squatted on either side of the street on the outskirts of town, then drifted into the middle of the place where a small square, formed by the intersection of the two main trails, one leading out to the plains and the other up into the hills, formed almost the exact centre of El Amaro. Here there were taller, two-storey buildings, the bank on one corner of the square, a saloon and a grain store at two others, and on the fourth, nearest to him, was a hotel, a wide veranda running around the outside of the entire building.

Beyond the hotel, almost forming a part of the same building, was a livery stable. A man drifted out of the dimness of the stable's rear darkness and came close to him taking the reins of the horse as Dane dropped lightly from the saddle. There was an unlit smoke between the man's lips and he stared up at the tall man through rheumy eyes. But there was, Dane noticed, a speculative gleam at the back of them and he saw the man place his hand on the sweat-gummed back of the horse, nodding a little to himself.

'This the only hotel in town?' he asked, nodding towards the nearby building.

'Reckon we're lucky to have that one, mister,' grinned the other. 'El Amaro ain't a big place as yuh c'n see. Don't get many visitors hereabouts.'

'Then I reckon I won't have any difficulty gettin' a room.' Dane moved away. The groom watched him for a moment through narrowed eyes, rubbed a hand over his stubbled chin, then led the horse away into one of the stalls at the back of the stables. Outside the hotel, Dane paused and rolled himself a cigarette. The smoke helped to ease a little of the tension running in his mind. Had his picture been sent on to this out-of-the-way place? he wondered. He would have liked to have talked with the sheriff about those men who had tried to kill Maller. The lawman seemed the obvious choice in town.

★ ★ ★

Sheriff Keeler came to the door of his office and stared out along the street into the darkness, just as the small group of riders turned into the main street and came towards him. He caught a glimpse of them in the light that came from the saloon, but he had not needed that glimpse to know that it was Ed Skinner and some of his crew. They reined their mounts in front of the office and Skinner climbed down, tossed the reins over the hitching bar, then strode purposefully on to the boardwalk, stopped in front of him.

'I'd like a word with yuh, Keeler,' he said brusquely. 'In yore office.'

Keeler sighed. 'I was just on my way to supper, Skinner,' he said harshly. 'Couldn't we talk there, in the hotel?'

For a moment, the other turned his gaze on the tall building at the corner of the square, then shook his head. 'Reckon not, Sheriff. This is private and there may be too many there.'

Keeping his temper with an effort, Keeler turned and led the way back into the office. As he closed the door behind him, the rest of Skinner's crew climbed down from their mounts and made their way across to the saloon.

Skinner lowered himself into the chair in front of the desk and waited with a deliberate show of impatience while the sheriff moved around and sat down. In the yellow light of the lamp, his face looked old and strained, but there was still a little of the ramrod erectness in his body and the set of the curling moustache that came from service in the Confederate Army during the War.

'Well, Mr Skinner. Suppose you tell me what's on your mind this time.'

'Yuh know as well as I do what's on my mind. That sodbuster Maller!'

'What's he done now?' Keeler had no liking whatever for the nesters who were trying to move in and take over the best land in the territory; but on the other hand, he wasn't sure that he liked Ed Skinner. The cattleman was a troublemaker and sooner or later he would precipitate this whole country into a range war, which was the one thing Keeler was trying to avoid. He was only too acutely aware that it was the cattlemen's money and their votes that put, and kept, him in office and they depended on him to take care of things and see that the law went in one way, covering up for them whenever one of the nesters was found shot on the open range, or there was a burning of their farms or barns. To be sure, the cattlemen asked for nothing in return, except that he should use the badge on his shirt as a means of seeing that the nesters were run off this range by any means at all, legal or not. It was a very nice setup indeed — for the cattlemen and the killers they had in their crews. More than half of the men who worked for these bosses and ranchers were wanted somewhere or other by the law.

'Maller is behind this attempt to drive us off the range. I've got all the proof I need. I took some of the boys with me this morning to bring him into town for trial, but he made a run for it when I caught him in the valley. We'd have strung him up for sure if some drifter hadn't butted in and forced us at gunpoint to turn him loose.'

'Drifter?' Keeler's eyes opened a

shade wider. 'Any idea who he was — or where he was headed?'

'After Maller, I reckon,' gritted the other. 'Now Maller is goin' to be doubly careful. We had the one chance to finish him, and we lost it because of this *hombre* who came puttin' his nose in where it wasn't wanted.'

'So what do you want me to do?' inquired the sheriff.

'I want this drifter found and run out of the territory. He can take any point of the compass he likes, so long as he keeps on ridin'.'

'Sounds as though he won't be an easy man to frighten,' muttered the other. He got heavily to his feet, scratching his chin thoughtfully. 'You know him if you saw him again?'

'I'd know him if I saw him in hell,' grated Skinner.

'All right. You take your men back to your place and leave this to me. I'll make inquiries, especially at Maller's place and around town.'

'I'll start askin' some questions of my

own,' Skinner told him tightly. 'I want this *hombre* out of the territory or put somewhere where he can cause no more trouble for me. I'm goin' to see that he doesn't stop me again.'

'Careful, Skinner,' warned the other. 'I know you figure you've got the law on your side, but I'll have to stop you if you start makin' any false moves, you know.'

'I just don't give a damn about yore threats, Keeler. Remember who put yuh into office. Without us cattlemen, yuh won't be sheriff.'

'I know all about that, Skinner.' Keeler nodded heavily, his gaze not leaving the other's face. 'But I'm the law in these parts, whether you like it or not, and I'll see that somethin' like this is run my way.'

For a moment, Skinner sat there, bereft of speech, then he pushed back his chair, got to his feet and stamped heavily and angrily to the door. Pausing, he turned. 'I'll give yuh forty-eight hours, Keeler. Then I'll be doin' things my way and to hell with the law.' He went out, slamming the door behind him. Sighing, Keeler went back to his desk and lowered his spare, gangling frame into the chair. He bit his lower lip fiercely and mentally cursed Ed Skinner and his crew of gunslingers. He felt curiously helpless. Most of the day had been spent riding the hill trails, feeling things out. He felt certain that something was going to break here and very soon, and there seemed nothing he could do to prevent it. The trouble was that deep down, he knew that Skinner was right. He was only a figurehead when it came to the law in this town. El Amaro was a cattle town, had been from the day it had been founded before the war; and cattlemen had run it their way for as long as he could remember. Now the nesters were spreading in from the east, bringing their own ways with them, armed with pieces of paper which said that they had a legal right to the land they claimed and the law was to provide them with all of the necessary protection in the event of trouble. Certainly the Government had foreseen that there was bound to be trouble between the settlers and the cattlemen. When a man grazed his cattle on a certain spread of land for more than twenty years, he considered that he had certain rights to it; and he took it ill when a bunch of sodbusters from back east suddenly turned up and turned him off it.

It was a grim business. Grim and cold. No quarter was asked between the two groups and none given. No mercy. Soon, it would either develop into a fight to the finish, or the Government would be forced to step in and enforce the laws it had made. He sighed, rolled a smoke and sat back in his chair for a long while, trying to think things out in his mind. Then, presently, he got up, locked the office and went over to the hotel for supper. It was there, in the dining-room, that he first caught sight of Dane Averill, seated at one of the tables in the corner of the room.

2

Cattlemen's Range

Sheriff Keeler hesitated in the doorway of the diner, then shrugged and walked in, strode over to the table in the corner where he paused and looked down at Dane, eyes narrowed like chips of flint.

'Stranger, were you out in the valley this mornin'?'

Dane lifted his head, noticed the star on the other's shirt and motioned with his knife towards the vacant chair opposite him. 'Take the weight off your feet, Sheriff,' he said casually. 'Now, what can I do for you?'

'I asked you a question, mister.' The deep-set eyes flickered over Dane, at the moment not too interested, as if the other recognized that there might be plenty of strangers riding into El Amaro and this might not be the man he sought. Still, there was a chance and the other looked like the kind of man who could handle a gun and might step into an argument between Maller and that bunch of headstrong cowpokes.

'All right, Sheriff. I came through the valley this morning. I suppose you want to ask me about the little ruckus there.' Dane felt a little prick of inward irritation but tried not to show it. 'I did mean to come over and talk with you about it as soon as I'd eaten my supper.'

'Any objection if I have mine while we talk?' asked the other.

'Reckon not. Saves trouble.' Dane continued to eat while the sheriff signalled to the waiter, gave his order, then sat back, watching him closely. When the lawman's meal arrived, he ate with relish for several minutes without speaking, then looked up. 'Just had a long parley with Ed Skinner. He came complainin' that you'd stepped in at a little party he and the boys were givin' this mornin'.'

'Yeah,' said Dane thinly. His brows drew together. 'And I'd do the same again if I had to.'

'Sometimes it ain't wise to butt into things like this.' The sheriff's eyes narrowed until they were almost shut, mere slits in his head.

With an effort, Dane held on to his temper. Outwardly, he looked cool and comparatively unruffled, but inside his temper flared and boiled. This was only going to confirm his earlier suspicions, that in a cattle town like El Amaro, the sheriff was on the side of the men who put him into power and kept him there. He certainly wasn't going to stick out his neck for any sodbuster, even if murder was being committed.

'Seems to me it's quite obvious where your sympathies lie,' muttered Averill tightly. 'Just who put you into this job of keepin' law and order here — Ed Skinner and his men?' Thinning his lips, Dane went on: 'You're playing a game here that's goin' to blow right up in your face before you know where you are. El Amaro is a powder keg, Sheriff, with a slow fuse, but there ain't much of that fuse left still to burn.'

Keeler breathed loudly through his mouth. For a moment, he seemed incapable of speaking, then he said sharply: 'You seem to know a hell of a lot about El Amaro, mister. If you're thinkin' of going' up against Skinner and his crew, then you'll be dead before you can make any more trouble for me.'

'Listen, Sheriff,' said Dane. 'If you ran into a bunch of cowpokes ready to hang a man, what would you do about it? Just sit by and watch it happen? Or get in there and try to stop 'em?'

'You don't know these nesters, stranger. They come here with pieces of paper that gives them the deeds to land which had been used as rangeland for more than fifty years. Do you wonder that the cattlemen are incensed. Barbed wire strung up along the trails and even over the ranges!'

'That so?' muttered Dane thinly. His tone was insolent and meant to be.

'Yeah, that's so,' snapped the other, getting riled up a little. 'I don't want no trouble in El Amaro and I aim to see there ain't any. You here for a reason or just ridin' through?'

Dane pursed his lips. 'I might stick around for a while, especially if I find what I'm lookin' for.'

'If you're aiming to start any trouble, then better forget it. I'll run you into the jail the first wrong move you make in my territory.'

'Reckon the first folk you ought to run into jail ought to be those killers who tried to string a man up this mornin'.' said Dane pointedly.

'I'll decide who's goin' to be jailed.' The other scraped back his chair and got to his feet. 'You makin' any charge against these men?'

'Nope.' Dane shook his head. Quietly, he added: 'Could be that Maller will when he gets around to thinkin' about this.'

Keeler said nothing, but his eyes were bleak, filled with cold anger. 'You just watch yourself while you're in town, mister,' he grunted. 'And stay away from Skinner and his bunch if you know what's good for you.'

Dane grinned, almost mockingly. 'Sheriff, I'm a peaceable man. I don't aim to cause any trouble. But if anybody tries to crowd me then they may find that they've bitten off a little more'n they can chew.'

'Now I've told you this ain't your range, mister. You strike me as a saddletramp, a trouble-maker. I don't want you in my town if that's right and so far you've done nothin' to make me change my mind about that. Understand — you've got no business here.'

Dane shook his head slowly. The mocking smile was still on his lips, but there was a hardness in his eyes. 'That's where you're wrong, Sheriff,' he said tightly. 'I do have business here.'

The sheriff stopped at that. He drew in his breath and let it out softly. 'Then I reckon I'd like to hear about it.'

'It's not good business, it's bad. I'm

lookin' for a man — and when I find him, whether it's in town or out there on the range someplace, I mean to kill him.'

Keeler stared hard at the other for a long while, his lips stretched tight and very thin. His eyes changed a little. The bleakness went out of them and something else came into their depths. Then he whirled on his heel and walked out of the diner, out through the small lobby of the hotel and into the dark and quiet street.

Inwardly, he felt sorely troubled. His mind whirled with confused thoughts as he strode over to his office, unlocked the door, went inside and lighted the oil lamp on the table before sitting down in his chair behind the desk. Just who was this stranger who had come riding into El Amaro looking for trouble and making it so gosh-darned obvious? There was a look about him that tagged him for a drifter, a saddle bum just keeping one step ahead of the law. Maybe it would be better to check through his collection of wanted posters when he had a little more time to make sure. There had been that look in the other's eyes which foreboded trouble — big trouble — in El Amaro; and that was one thing he, the sheriff, didn't want. Not with Ed Skinner moving in on Maller and the other settlers, hankering to run them out of the territory in spite of their Government grants and deeds.

Back in the diner, Dane finished his supper, sat back in his chair and rolled a cigarette. He felt relaxed and satisfied. The meal had been a good one, plenty to eat, and the food well cooked. But in a way it had acted as a stimulant rather than something that sated his appetite, making him feel drowsy. Restlessness bubbled up in his mind and when he finally got up from the table and made his way outside, little pictures of the past weeks came back into his mind, bringing his brows together until lines of shrewdness formed on his brow. Maybe the inward urges of a lone man always moved like this whenever he was hunting down a man who had done him a great wrong. The feeling of vengeance was a strong driving force that made a man do things he would not normally have done.

He made his way to the livery stable, watered his horse then strode over to the saloon. A small group of men saddled up and rode away as he approached and in the darkness, he heard their coarse laughter and wild shouts, fading as they rode north out of town. Giving the street a careful study, he paused, then pushed open the doors of the saloon and stepped inside. The saloon was big, but there was no ventilation and cigarette smoke hung heavily in the air, forming a blue haze over the tables. There were other smells there too, cheap whiskey and the sweat of men who had ridden hard. Here and there, men played cards at the tables or lounged against the walls and along the narrow bar which stretched from one side of the room to the other.

One thing Dane noticed in a swift, all-embracing glance. There was not a solitary sodbuster in the whole saloon. These were cattlemen, some drifters and others evidently out-and-out gunmen, hired by the big ranchers to protect their interests. Dane felt a distinct prickle run along the hairs on the nape of his neck as he noticed the two men standing at the bar, their backs to him, faces averted a little. He knew them both instantly as two of the men he had met in the valley — Ed Skinner's men. There was no sign of the big boss himself. Maybe he was in town, trying to get the sheriff to back what he had tried to do that morning. Dane made his way over to the bar in a leisurely manner, glanced up as the white-coated bartender came in his direction.

'What'll it be, mister?'

'Beer,' said Dane softly. He took up his position at the bar where he could watch the two men on one side of him. The bartender was a little slow in the way he brought the beer over and when he set the glass down on the counter in front of him, there was a sudden, worried frown on his face.

'Seems like you ain't got any sense at all, mister,' muttered the taller of the two men at the bar. 'You should've kept on ridin' while you had the chance.'

'This your town?' cut in Dane softly. 'I aim to ride where I please.'

The other stiffened and set his half-empty glass down on the bar in front of him, half turning. The bartender edged away, muttered: 'Now what is all this, gents? I don't want any gunplay here. If you've got to fight somethin' out between yourselves, take it outside into the street.'

'This is a nester-lover,' snapped the big man harshly. His face reddened a little, eyes narrowed to slits. 'Rode in and stopped us stringin' up that *hombre* Maller this mornin'. Reckon we ought to ask him a few questions, boys. Like where he comes from and what he's doin' here in El Amaro.'

There was a mutter of approval for this. Several of the men at the tables eyed Dane curiously, all hostile. Dane gave no sign of noticing. He had been in plenty of ticklish, precarious positions before and he knew these two men who faced him were ripe for mischief, ready for trouble.

'I ain't answerin' any of your questions,' Dane said quietly. 'I just don't like to see a man bein' hanged without a trial, especially when it looks to me as though he's never had a chance to defend himself.'

The big man stepped forward a couple of paces and his right hand hung dangerously close to his gun. 'Mister, you butted in back there when it was none of your business. You shot two of our boys and let that critter, Maller, escape. Ed Skinner don't like that. Reckon he's goin' to be mighty pleased to have a word with you right now.'

The other was watching Dane much in the same way that a rattler watches a rabbit, with unblinking eyes, waiting for him to make a move, confident that he was faster than the other and that this time, Dane would not be able to draw on him unnoticed. Casually, Dane reached out for his drink and drained the glass, setting it down on the bar. He could see the look of fear on the barkeep's face.

'You figuring on takin' me to Skinner?' asked Dane, slow and easy. Even as he spoke, the other cowhand moved away from the bar, away from his companion, spreading out in a well-planned move so that the two of them might take him from the sides. A table was overturned as the men at it pushed it out of their way, got to their feet and moved over to the far wall, out of the line of fire.

There was a tight, thin-lipped grin on the taller man's face as he sneered: 'This is where you get it, stranger. I've been waiting to get an even chance at you. That was a fluke draw you made on us this mornin'.'

Dane moved slowly away from the

bar, his hands hanging loosely by his sides, his eyes deliberately unfocused, so that he could watch either man at the same time. He knew that both of these men would be trained, professional killers, picked for their speed with the gun. But there had been a faint edge to the big man's voice which showed to Dane's keen ears that he was not as sure of himself as he tried to make everyone believe.

'You're scared,' he said softly. Dane's cold eyes flickered from one man to the other. 'You're not quite sure of this, even though there are two of you . . . '

'Draw when you're ready, damn you!' roared the big man, his voice dry.

'Now let's have no shootin' in here,' called the bartender. He stood with his hands on the bar, but Dane guessed there was a shot-gun somewhere behind it and the other was only waiting for a chance to reach down and grab it. He wasn't sure just whose side the bartender was on. The Skinner boys seemed to be big men in El Amaro,

Skinner himself would be one of the top men who gave the orders and it was unlikely that small fry such as this barkeep would want to go against him. Dane grinned tightly. He could visualise a gun load of buckshot hammering into his back as soon as either of the men in front of him went for his gun.

A moment later, he saw the growing light of action in the big man's eyes. There was an instant's hardening of the other's face. Then his hands swept down towards his guns with the speed of a striking rattler. At the same moment, his companion threw himself sideways and went clawing for his own guns. Dane scarcely seemed to move. One moment his hands were empty, the next the twin Colts were balanced in the palms of his fists and the guns roared in the saloon. Both men yelled loud and long, went reeling back, one nursing a smashed shoulder and the other holding a bloodied hand from which the gun had been sent spinning across the room. The levelled guns in

Dane's hands oozed smoke. Then he carefully refilled the empty chambers and, thrust the Colts back into their holsters with the easy, casual movements of a man who knew there would be no further trouble.

'Better get the doc to take a look at 'em both,' said a man from near the wall. 'Don't figure they'll be doin' much more ridin' or shootin' for Skinner, for a little while.'

Someone went out through the swing doors. Scarcely had they closed behind him then they were pushed open again and the sheriff came barging into the saloon, his eyes taking in everything in a single, sweeping glance. He had his Colt in his right hand and he stiffened abruptly as his gaze swung from the two wounded cowhands to Dane.

'I figured you'd be involved in this as soon as I heard the shootin' from along the street,' he said tightly. 'What happened in here?'

'See for yourself, Sheriff,' said Dane quietly. 'These men drew on me and I was forced to shoot 'em.'

Slowly, the sheriff lowered the gun to his side, then thrust it back into its holster. 'Reckon I ought to take you in, stranger,' he said thinly. 'I warned you that you'd do somethin' bad for this town — and by thunder, you've just done it.'

'Wounded a couple of the killers who ride this part of the territory,' said Dane softly. 'Reckon that because they ride for Skinner that makes all the difference.'

'Just keep your mouth shut, mister — and leave me to ask the questions,' said the other tautly. 'You say they drew on you first. Don't seem right to me.'

'No? You figure they were just spread out like that for nothin'? Could be, of course, that everybody in this saloon is a mite scared of Ed Skinner and will testify that I drew first.' He made to say something further but at that moment the swing doors opened and a short, fussy little man with grey side whiskers came in carrying the black bag that marked him as the town doctor.

'Guess you'll both be out of commission for a little while, three or four weeks at the least,' he said to the man with the shoulder wound. Then he went over to the other. 'As for you, Clem, that shot has busted up your hand pretty bad. Reckon you won't be usin' that to shoot with any more.'

'Hell, doc, can't you give me something for the pain,' gritted the other harshly. His voice rasped from a dry throat.

'Sure, sure, I'll give you something,' the doctor nodded his head, then grunted. There was a faintly mocking smile on his whiskered features as he said: 'Reckon this time you met up with somebody whose draw is a mite faster than your own.'

'Shut your mouth, doc, and just get on with what you have to do.'

'You say these two men started this fracas?' said the sheriff, turning to Dane. There was a curious look on his face, a blend of anger and frustration.

'That's right, Sheriff. These are two of the bunch who were trying to hang that fella this morning.'

The other's eyes narrowed. He said harshly. 'My advice to you, mister, is to get back to your room at the hotel, stay there, and be on the first stage in the mornin'. That way, you might be able to steer clear of trouble.'

Dane shook his head slowly. 'Like I told you earlier, Sheriff, I'm here to find a man. When I've found him and finished my business with him, then I might consider ridin' on.'

Turning, he made his way out of the saloon and into the street. The air was cool and clear after the hot, stuffy atmosphere of the saloon and he drew in great lungfuls of it, feeling it go down into his body like wine. Overhead, the sky was brilliant and clear, with a thousand bright stars gleaming so sharply that it seemed all one had to do was reach up and touch them with an outstretched hand. The moon had not yet risen and there was only the faint gleam of starshine and the swathes of light that shone from the windows of the buildings fronting the street. But most of the street lay in pools of deep shadow. Narrow alleys led off from it at intervals, dark, gaping mouths of blackness that showed between the squat buildings and stores.

It was as he was passing level with one of these that he heard the faint movement in the pitch blackness of the alley. Instantly, he swung round, hand dropping towards the gun at his belt, but his fingertips had barely brushed the butt when a hard voice said: 'Hold it right there, mister.'

The hidden rider urged his mount out of the shadows where he had evidently been waiting for a long while. There was a rifle in his hands, held steady on Dane's chest. It was Ed Skinner.

'Been wonderin' where I seen your face before,' said the other tightly. 'Then it came to me a little while ago. You're Dane Averill. There's a reward out for you, dead or alive.'

'And you aim to collect?'

The other pursed his lips. 'Just heard that you shot two more of my boys back there in the saloon. Now that wasn't very smart. I run things around here and I don't like anybody who comes ridin' in and tryin' to hinder me in any way like you did. Maybe this mornin' you didn't know what the score was between the cattlemen and the nesters. Now you do. We aim to run 'em all out of the territory and those who don't run, we shoot and bury up yonder on Boot Hill. They can have their choice. But I figure that maybe we ought to have a necktie party for you. After I've handed you over to the sheriff and collected the reward, of course.' There was now a sneering grin on the other's face.

For a moment, Dane's hand moved a little towards the gun at his hip. He cursed himself for not having had his wits about him, for walking into this trap like a blind tinhorn.

'Try it,' snapped the other, noticing the movement. 'The reward is payable for you, dead or alive. Don't matter much to me which you are.'

Clearly the other wanted him to go for his gun, knowing that he had the drop on him, could shoot him down there in the street without any danger to himself. A dark anger suffused the older man's face and his finger tightened on the trigger of the rifle. 'I'm goin' to kill you, Averill.' It was simply said but each word carried the promise of death within the next few moments. 'I don't know what your business is here in El Amaro, but whatever it is, it's goin' to stop right here and now.'

'You reckon that you'll get away with this — even here, with the sheriff on your side?' said Dane thinly. He spaced his words out, sharp and distinct.

The other's lips drew back in a sneer. 'I'll get away with it all right. Said you tried to go for your gun when I stopped you. I've only got to show that wanted poster with your picture on it, and nobody is goin' to ask any awkward questions.'

There seemed to be no sound, no movement in the dark street now. Dane tensed himself, watching the dark eyes that stared without pity into his own, knew that he had only seconds in which to live, that whatever happened, no matter how futile it seemed, he would have to try to throw himself to one side, to jerk out his own weapon and use it. Skinner drew a rasping breath deep into his lungs, let it go again in jerky gasps. Dane's eyes locked with Skinner's. Waiting, watching, probing for the sign which would tell him that death was on its way. The other lifted the long barrel of the rifle, sighted it calmly on Dane's chest. A single pressure on the trigger and Dane would be dead. Desperately, he tensed himself to drop to one side, saw Skinner grin fiercely.

Then sharply, crisply, a woman's voice rang out from the shadows on the boardwalk at the far side of the alley mouth. Hard and commanding, the sound jerked Skinner up in his saddle brought Dane's head swinging round swiftly.

'Drop that rifle, Skinner, or I'll kill you.'

For a moment, there was indecision on the man's face. Then he thought better of any action he had considered taking, let the rifle fall with a clatter from his fingers, lips drawn into a hard, tight line. The girl came forward from the shadows and Dane watched her with surprise. She was tall for a woman, would have come well above his shoulder, he thought, with auburn hair that glistened a little in the dim light. Her wide-brimmed hat was pushed well back on her head so that the curls showed under it. She might have been nineteen, possibly in her twenties, it was difficult to tell in the dimness. But there was no mistaking the deadly purpose of the gun she had in her hand.

Dane took a slow, deep breath, moved forward. The girl watched him with a direct and speculative expression, barely showing interest. Yet she had stepped in and saved his life when there had been no need for her to get mixed up in this business at all.

'You're makin' a big mistake buttin' in like this,' said Skinner. 'While you're in town, my boys can drop you from any street corner. Remember that. I've got no quarrel with you, only with your father, but if you want to save this *hombre's* life, then you're makin' it your business and you'll have to be ready to take the consequences.'

The girl's eyes turned darker and her self-confidence seemed suddenly more bitter than before. 'I ought to shoot you where you are, Skinner,' she said in a low, menacing tone. 'Now ride, or I'll pull this trigger.'

Skinner sat tall in the saddle for a long moment, his mouth working, his face purpling with anger. Then he pulled hard on the reins, wheeled his mount sharply and spurred it out into the street, swinging north. The girl turned and watched him until he had gone out of sight, then slowly lowered the gun, her hand falling to her side. She suddenly seemed to have exhausted the source of energy that had kept her facing Skinner during those past few moments.

'I'm glad you turned up when you did, Miss — ' Dane hesitated.

'I'm Victoria Maller,' said the girl quietly. She thrust the gun into its holster, turned and whistled shrilly. A few moments later a palomino came trotting slowly from the shadows further along the street.

'Victoria Maller!' Dane spoke her name more sharply than he had intended, surprise putting an edge to his tone. Slowly, he nodded his head in understanding and went on: 'I met your father this mornin'. Skinner and some of his men were set on hanging him when I rode up. I reckon you've just repayed any debt there might have been on your father's part.'

For a moment, fear showed in the

girl's eyes and she was suddenly not as self-confident as she had been a few moments before when she had faced Ed Skinner. 'Is my father all right?' she asked quickly.

Dane grinned. 'He was when I last saw him. Reckoned he could fight off all of Skinner's men if they tried to attack him on the home spread.'

The girl's glance was worried. She gave him a deep, studying glance and for a moment something seemed balanced in her mind; then she shrugged her shoulder and swung herself easily into the saddle. She made a small motion with her right hand as she said softly 'You'll have to be more careful in town. This place is nothing but eyes and ears and everything gets back to Skinner. You'll always be watched and they'll kill you whenever they get a chance.' A pause while she eyed him closely. 'You don't look like the usual saddletramp who comes riding through this town. Why don't you get your horse and ride on, head over the hills, and keep on riding?'

'Could be I'll do just that; once I've finished some business here in El Amaro.'

'Be careful you're not killed before you get a chance to finish that business,' murmured the girl. 'Skinner will stop at nothing to get what he wants.'

'Don't you think that applies to you as well, Miss Maller?'

The girl smiled, but there was little mirth in it. 'I can take care of myself, when it comes to men like Skinner,' she said positively. 'There are men in town I can trust.'

'Mebbe so, but it seems to me that the law is working in cahoots with the cattlemen around here.'

'Sheriff Keeler, you mean,' nodded the girl. Her eyes were shadowed to him and he could not see the expression in them. 'He's only in office so long as the cattlemen say so. He knows it — and so does everyone else in town. Only time he ever takes a posse out is when he tries to hunt down this outlaw gang who've been holding up the freight and rustling cattle from every rancher in the territory.'

'Outlaws! Rustlers?' Dane gave her a bright, sharp stare.

'That's right.' The girl gave a quick nod. 'Somebody is leading them who knows everything that goes on in town. Somebody who knows when a gold shipment is leaving or when one of the ranchers means to move some of his prime beef off the range, ready to drive to market.'

'How do you know the Sheriff ain't workin' hand in glove with them too?'

'I don't. But it isn't likely. Skinner has been robbed of more than two thousand head in the past few months and the other ranchers are the same.'

Dane grinned tightly. 'That's the oldest game in the world. Rustle your own cattle so no one will suspect you.'

'Maybe you're right,' agreed the girl. She sat tall in the saddle for a long moment, staring down at him. 'You're sure my father is all right?'

'Sure. That is, if he spoke the truth when he said Skinner and his men wouldn't dare attack him on his own land.'

Victoria Maller seemed satisfied at that. She remained silent for a long while, sitting with her hands resting on the pommel of the saddle. She looked into the cool darkness of the town and her face seemed sober and indrawn. When she spoke again, there was the drag of sadness and concern in her voice. 'We came out here expecting the Government to enforce the laws it made, to make sure that we were allowed to farm our land in peace. But first the cattlemen and now these outlaws seem determined to drive us away. I don't know what brought my father here and I don't know what he wants out of this country. It can be both beautiful and cruel. But men do many things for many reasons a lot of them foolish. But they are men's reasons and I don't pretend to understand them. But if you came riding here for vengeance, to kill a man — and that seems to be the only motive that brings any man to a place like El Amaro — then you're a fool. You saw how easy it was for Skinner to get the drop on you back there.'

'It won't happen again,' Dane said.

The girl regarded him closely for another long moment, then touched spurs to her mount. There had been that strangely speculative look in her eyes as she had ridden off and he stood for a while in the deep shadows of the boardwalk, staring after her. His mind was a confused whirling of thoughts. Not so much that the girl had saved his life, that she had told him of the outlaw band in this part of the country. One expected these thing on the frontier where the old ways of violence were slow to change. But because for the first time he had learned the name of the sheriff of this town. Sheriff Keeler. And the man he had ridden here to find, the man he had sworn to kill when he did meet him face to face, was named Clem Keeler!

He stood quite still in the shadows, then rolled himself a smoke, trying to put his thoughts into some kind of order in his mind. There was the feeling that perhaps his long search was over, that El Amaro was the last town on the trail for him. That brought with it a faint sense of satisfaction. Then there was the knowledge that the man he meant to kill was perhaps the sheriff's son. That complicated matters a lot. And what about the girl? Where did she and her father fit into all this? She had not seemed afraid when she had faced up to Ed Skinner with that gun in her hand, and the demeanour had indicated that she would have used it without compunction if the necessity had arisen. And she had not seemed in the least scared at the prospect of riding back to the valley after dark.

★　★　★

It was still dark when he woke in the room at the hotel. For a moment, he lay quite still, trying to recall the sound which had woken him. He could have been sleeping for hours, or perhaps only minutes, it was impossible to tell; but he did know that something had brought him awake and he suddenly sat up straight in the bed, straining his ears to pick out the sound again.

For a long while, he could hear nothing. A horse whinnied from somewhere down near the livery stable, but that was the only sound which disturbed the deep and clinging stillness. Maybe it had been nothing more than a dream, he reasoned, but it was not usual for him to dream and —

He slipped out of the low iron bed, went over to the window. He could just make out the narrow balcony that ran around the outside of the building, on a level with the window. Carefully, quietly, he pulled on his clothing, checked the guns in his holsters. A moment later, he heard the faint tapping on his door, a gentle sound as if whoever was there wanted to waken only him and nobody else in the hotel.

Puzzled, he walked forward, stood close to the door and asked in a low, harsh tone: 'Who's there? What do you want?'

'Mr Averill?'

He tried to pin the voice, but it was one he didn't recollect having heard before. Sliding one of the Colts from its holster, he turned the key softly in the lock, then jerked the door open. The door swung inward and Dane looked hard at the bearded oldster who stood there in the corridor . . . The old man grinned a red-gummed smile. He looked harmless enough, Dane thought, lowering the gun a little, but this could be a trap thought up by Skinner.

'You can put that gun away, mister. This is a friendly visit.'

'Maybe so,' grunted Dane. 'But I'm not used to friendly visits at this time of the night.'

'Listen, Mr Averill. I know why

you're here in this town. You're lookin' for a man, ain't you?'

'You seem to know a lot.' Dane put the gun back into its holster with an obvious reluctance. He couldn't make up his mind about this man. He could know something and he looked like the kind of man nobody would bother about; harmless and consequently on nobody's side. A man who sat around town and saw and heard a lot without giving the impression that he was taking any notice.

'I see everythin' that goes on in El Amaro. This is one hell of a town, as you probably know. What with Skinner tryin' to stir up the cattlemen against the nesters; and that outlaw bunch riding the hills and stoppin' all freight whenever there might be a load of gold on board, things can be pretty hot.'

'I'll bet they can,' Dane ground out. 'But I don't see where that concerns me. I want no part of any feuds that might be goin' on around here. Looks to me like there's a full-scale range war workin' itself up.

The old man grinned tightly. 'You're in it whether you like it or not, mister. They reckon you've been buckin' Ed Skinner and that's bad. Once you've sided with the nesters, you're as good as dead.'

'Then where do you fit in?' asked Dane, curious. He was trying to hold down the tight feeling of apprehension that threatened to engulf him.

'Let's say I don't like the way Skinner and the other ranchers act. I've seen what they do to the nesters and from what I've heard, you're the sort of man who might be able to stand up to 'em. Besides, I happen to know where you can find Clem Keeler.'

'He the sheriff's son?'

'That's right. Pretty bad character. You ain't the only one who'd like to kill him, not if the others knew as much about him as I do.'

Dane's eyes narrowed. He took a step towards the other, gripped him by the front of the shirt, bunching it in his fist.

He had half suspected that Keeler might be the son of the lawman here in El Amaro. That complicated matters. 'What do you know about him?' he demanded harshly.

'He's lined up with those outlaws ridin' the hills,' said the other with a show of impatience. 'Ride up there and you're sure to find him.' The other cackled softly. 'That is, if he don't find you first.'

'And the sheriff?' asked Dane, surprised, 'does he know about this?'

'Don't see that he can,' retorted the other. 'If he does, he ain't made no show of it. He still takes the posse out huntin' these *hombres* down whenever the stage or one of the freight wagons is held up. Don't figger he'd do that if he knew his son was leadin' them critters.'

'No, you're right, old-timer.' Dane breathed. He released his hold on the other, stared off into the dimness of the room. 'But these hills are the best part of a hundred miles long and thirty miles deep. How d'you reckon one man could cover all that territory, especially if the sheriff can't do it with all of his men. He knows this country better than I do.'

The old man's eyes glittered brightly. 'I see a lot and I know a lot that goes on around here. I know much more'n I ever tell anybody. Nobody here I could trust anyways. If I told what I know to the sheriff or Ed Skinner, I wouldn't be an old man, I'd be a dead one. I guess I'm the only one in town who could lead you to their hide-out in the hills.'

Dane felt the tightness grow in him suddenly. 'You've got some reason for doin' this,' he said finally. 'What is it?'

The other straightened, looked pained. Then he bent forward a little. 'Could be I've been waitin' for somebody I knew I could trust to ride into town and I heard you were lookin' for this man.'

Dane's eyes narrowed to slits. 'How did you know that?' he demanded harshly.

Again there was the toothy grin. 'I

was in the shadows watchin' when you talked to Miss Victoria.' The man nodded his head wisely. 'I reckoned you were finished when Skinner got the drop on you.'

'So that's it.' Dane looked at the other with a little more respect. He had never suspected the other's presence. As far as he had been aware, the entire street had been empty. And yet this man had been crouched there in the black shadows, so close that he had been able to pick out every word they had spoken.

'I'm glad you weren't gunnin' for me, old-timer.'

'That mean you're interested in ridin' out into the hills after coyotes?' he asked.

Dane glanced at the other with a moment's penetrating attention, then nodded as he said. 'Just when were you figuring on riding out there?'

'No time like the present,' grunted the other. 'Ain't nobody watchin' the trail right now and there are a few hours of darkness left. Too many men keepin' watch along the hill trails in daylight.'

Dane hesitated for a moment. The feeling of danger was still strong within him but he shrugged it away. The other seemed to be telling the truth and one thing was certain, he seemed to know a lot about what was going on in this hell-town. If it was a trap, then the other would go first, he promised himself.

They went out into the silent corridor, down the creaking stairs and out through the lobby of the hotel. There was no one behind the desk and Dane knew now how the other had managed to get to him without being seen or heard. Then they were out in the night and the cool air washed away the sleep from Dane's mind and he was able to think more clearly. By the faint light of the half moon, hanging low over the two-storied houses, he was able to make out the horse that stood patiently in front of the hitching rail.

'Your mount in the livery stables?' muttered the other softly.

Dane nodded slowly. He made his way along the dusty street, eyes alert, probing the shadows that lay thick and huge on either side. In front of him, the main street stretched away into the darkness like a faintly glowing ribbon of silver where the pale wash of moonlight fell on it.

Dane saw no one in the stables as he went inside, found his mount in one of the stalls at the rear and led it out into the street. The whole town seemed to be asleep, but it was an uneasy sleep, as if everyone there slept with one hand on their gun, ready to come awake at the slightest provocation. Carefully, he swung himself up into the saddle, waited for the other to join him. They rode out to the west of the town, into the darkness. Squat houses lay on either side of them as they moved through the outskirts of El Amaro. Then these fell behind and they were on a rocky part of the trail that led upwards into higher ground, overlooking the plateau on which the town stood. Glancing back, Dane saw the whole town laid out behind them, but not a single light showed and the pale ribbon of the main street lay empty and silent, where it wound its way through the middle of town.

3

Trail of Fury

Along the trail to the west of town, the ground was barren and open, unlike that along which Dane had ridden the previous day. It seemed scarcely credible that such different types of country could lie so close to the same town and yet here, he could see, even in the pale moonlight, no man had ever been able to tame this land. It seemed to lie covered under the flooding moonlight, with pale dust lying over everything and harshly-etched rocks rising up at every turn. The clatter of their horses' hoofs on the ground had a strangely metallic ring that was grating on the ears, setting the teeth and nerves on edge. They topped a low rise a quarter of an hour after riding out of town and in front of them was a stretching territory, a land of distances so vast that it was impossible to take in everything in a single glance. There were immense buttes swelling from the flat prairie far to the north-west, undulating mounds of rock and sandstone that drifted into obscurity where the eye could not reach in the dimness.

Dane let his glance drift ahead of him as he rode, content for the moment to trust the old man who rode beside him. This type of country would never allow the grazing of cattle and he doubted if even the nesters could make anything of it. It was too vast; it would take for ever to tame it, no matter how many men tried. Time was locked quite still here among the rocks and buttes and there were secret places which would always be there until the end of time for nothing, he felt sure, could ever make it anything else but what it was. But it was an ideal country in which men could hide from the law. The stage trail ran through here, across the arid desert and the hills crowded in on it from either side, making it easy for the outlaws to swoop down without any warning, take their loot and ride off again, hiding in the immensities of the hills, laughing at the law, ready to strike again whenever the opportunity came.

Fifteen minutes later, his companion reined his mount at a bend in the trail, held up his right hand. Dane stopped beside him, looked about him curiously.

'You're sure you know where you're goin'?' he asked hoarsely. 'There could be a thousand places where them men could hide.'

The other grinned. 'Didn't I tell you I could lead you right to 'em? You ain't doubtin' me, are you?'

Dane sighed. He shook his head, looked at the other with a steady regard that showed nothing of the thoughts which were going through his mind. He was beginning to think that the other knew very little, that he was leading him out here on a wild goose chase. Still, there was just the chance that the other did know something and at the moment, he himself had no lead to go on.

The old man leaned forward in his saddle, pointed directly ahead of him. 'The stage trail heads north yonder. You can just see it out there on the desert. But there's another trail leadin' up into the hills a little further on. That's the one we take. It gets pretty narrow higher up and you'll have to ride behind me and keep your horse under tight control.'

'All right,' Dane nodded quickly. He glanced at the sky overhead. It still wanted another two or three hours to dawn, he reckoned. They ought to be able to ride well into the hills before it was light enough for any look-outs to spot them.

The other gigged his mount forward, lips thinned. Five minutes later, they reached the point where the stage trail moved away into the plateau. To their left lay broken ground where no trail seemed to exist. Their horses picked their way carefully across it for perhaps a hundred yards, before they met up with a narrow trail that twisted up into the hills, looming high on their left. So the oldster had been right about this, Dane considered inwardly. Perhaps the other was on the right trail after all. He experienced a renewal of the tension in his mind, felt a little twitching of the hairs on the nape of his neck. So far, he hadn't considered what to do if the old man did lead him to this outlaw gang. It wasn't likely that they could take on the whole bunch with any chance of coming out of the ensuing gun battle alive.

The going got rougher as they climbed. Here and there, were spaces over which it seemed impossible they could cross, but the oldster pushed his mount forward fearlessly and Dane followed, guiding the bay with a tight rein. On their right, the rock wall fell sheer for close on a hundred feet, down into a wide, boulder-strewn valley. On their left, the bare ground rose steeply, forming an impassable barrier, leaving only a three-foot wide trail that twisted and wound its way upwards. And now a new menace added to their discomfort. A harsh, cold wind came sighing strongly down the mountain face, increasing in strength every minute. It hoarded up sharp, anguished sounds that shrieked at the ears and flung itself in their faces, bringing clouds of dust that stung their eyes and plugged their mouths and noses, forcing them to ride with their heads bowed, unable to see far in the pale moonlight. Dane pulled the collar of his jacket higher around his neck, tried to breathe more slowly as the grains of sand filtered into his mouth and throat.

The moon drifted behind a bank of dark cloud, the light died out and they were forced to make their way upward in almost pitch blackness. The feel of the mountain looming over him, was a constant pressure on Dane's mind, something he could not rid himself of no matter how hard he tried. All of those millions of tons of granite and rock, piled high above their heads, crushing down on them, made its presence felt even though, in the darkness, he could not see it. There was water flowing at the bottom of the canyon on their right now, he could hear it quite plainly and the cold, chill dampness of it began to rise up and engulf them, the sound it made rushing over its stony bed, increasing as they rode.

'How much further do we have to ride?' he asked, after a long silence.

The other's voice drifted back to him from the darkness. 'Not much further now. Used to be a settlement up here long before the war. Folk there got wiped out by Indians and it's been deserted since then. That's where these outlaws are hiding out. Leastways, they was a couple of month ago.'

'A couple of months.' In spite of himself, Dane could not keep in the sudden ejaculation. 'But they could have moved out any time since then, especially if things got hot for them around these parts. They could be anywhere by now.'

'They won't move from here unless they're forced,' called the other. He deliberately kept his head averted, rode low in the saddle as the icy wind blew down the steep slope.

Dane sat back in his saddle, defeated and full of exasperation. He had thought there might be something a little more positive about the other's promise to lead him to this gang's hideout. Now, it seemed, the other simply knew where they had been two months before. And judging from what the other's memory must be like at his age, his brain possibly a little befuddled, so that he could not tell one week from the other, it might have been far longer than that. He could see that his chances of meeting Clem Keeler face to face were diminishing swiftly.

Tightening his grip on the reins, he tried to peer into the darkness ahead of them. He could just make out the shape of the other and the narrow trail in front of him, but beyond that everything was vague and shadowy, strangely unreal in the darkness. He drew in a deep breath and let it go. The cliff wall seemed to be composed of rock and earth now, with some vegetation clinging precariously to it, growing out of narrow cracks where a little soil managed to exist in spite of the wind and dust. The horses were tired and doubtful on this trail, unsure of their footing, but the old man continued to press his to the limit as they rode from one canyon to another until at last, they rode into a levelling-off place, an area that had been roughened and blistered by some geological upheaval countless millions of years before and now stood before them like an oasis in this desert of rock.

The darkness gave Dane a feeling of comfort. He could see little, but the other seemed to know exactly where he was. After all, he had brought him this far, but whether the outlaws were still holed up in the settlement in these hills, he did not know.

'Yonder,' said the other in a hushed whisper. 'About a quarter of a mile away. There are two ways into the settlement and I reckon they will have both of 'em watched. We'll have to watch our step now.'

'Figure we'd better go the rest of the way on foot?' muttered Dane quietly.

He saw the other nod in the blackness. Sliding from the saddle, he lighted softly on the hard ground waited for the other. They moved forward, feeling their way among the upthrusting boulders, eyes straining into the pitch blackness. The first few drops of rain fell, spattering on to the rocks. A wall of rock lifted in front of them and he touched it with his outstretched hand. When he realized that his eyes had failed him, he felt a sudden twinge of uncertainty. They were now almost at the edge of the levelling-off plateau and somewhere in front of them, it was impossible to tell exactly where, he knew the ground would commence to drop once more, whether shallowly or steeply, he did not know. He bent forward, keeping close to the old-timer. For all his age, the other seemed as agile as a mountain goat and as silent.

'There's a fresh slide of dirt somewhere hereabouts,' muttered the other, stepping closer to him, his voice carrying for only a few feet. 'We'll have to work our way around it. This is the more difficult path, but the one they may not be watchin'.'

Dane nodded, stood up straight, easing the pincers of cramp in his legs. He used his hands for exploring, felt his fingers touch dirt; a wet spot on the cliff side that had given way recently, sending dirt and powdered rock cascading on to the narrow trail, As the other had said, it was a fresh slide, partially blocking the trail, the dirt not packed firm. He paused while the other worked his way forward, holding his breath, then letting it out in short pinches. He strained his ears to pick out the faintest sound, but nothing seemed to move in the vicinity and he began to feel a little easier in his mind. Maybe, after all, they might be able to take these *hombres* by surprise. The other slid around the side of the rock and Dane worked his way cautiously forward. The sound of water down below him in the canyon made a faint background noise in his ears and once, when his probing foot caught a piece of rock and sent it rattling over the side of the precipice, he heard it falling for what seemed an interminable time before the sound faded altogether and he still wasn't sure that the rock had hit the bottom of the steep slope. He felt a little tremor go through him, forced his mind away from the fact that death lay within a few inches of his slowly-moving feet. The oldster had made it safely and there was no reason why he shouldn't.

Moments later, he was on the other stretch of the trail, able to stand upright, drawing the cold air down into his lungs, feeling the sweat icily chill on his brow and the muscles of his back. The trail played on through gravel and tall chunks of rock. Halfway along it, the other halted suddenly, motioned Dane down. Crouching back against the rock, he peered into the darkness.

'Somethin' there,' murmured the other. 'I spotted him a second ago.'

Dane stared for a long moment, then shook his head. 'You sure?' he whispered. 'I don't see anythin'.'

'Hell, I ain't sure of nothin' in this darkness,' growled the other. 'But I'd swear there was somethin' there and — '

Seconds later, the moon broke loose of the ragged, trailing mass of black cloud, flooded the scene with light. Twenty yards away, there was the black mass of rock, a loose outline that seemed to lift from the trail itself and looking upwards, Dane clearly saw the silhouette of the man who stood on top of the rock, the rifle in his hands. It was too late for them to move back, the moonlight showed them both too clearly for the man to miss seeing them. With a quick movement, the man brought the rifle up to his shoulder and fired, the bullet striking wide of their position. Silence counted for nothing now. That single shot would have stirred up the whole hornet's nest.

'Get back to the horses while I hold them off,' he said thinly, tugging at the oldster's arm.

The other made to protest, then saw the force of Dane's argument and slipped past him as Dane brought the Colts hissing from their holsters. He snapped a couple of shots at the man on the rock as the other tried to get in another shot at them. The crack of the rifle was a harsh bark of sound. Then the guns in Dane's hands spoke. The man on the rock teetered for a moment, striving to hold himself upright; but first the rifle slipped from his nerveless grasp and bounced off the smooth rock and then his body bent in the middle as if he had been slammed in the stomach by a hard fist and he pitched off the rock, hit the trail and rolled inertly out of sight in the moon-thrown shadows.

Swiftly, without pausing to check whether any more of the men had moved up to join the look-out, Dane slipped back, around the slide of earth, not pausing this time, all fear gone in the knowledge that very soon, possibly within a minute or so, the rest of the outlaw band would be hot on their trail; and these men knew the hill trails far better than he did. His heart slammed against his ribs with the knowledge.

He exhaled and felt the dampness of sweat on the palms of his hands where they still gripped the revolvers. Beyond the slide, the twisting trail was empty and he breathed a sigh of thankfulness as he realized that the oldtimer had not paused to see what was happening behind him, but had done as he had been told, and moved back to the waiting horses as quickly as he could. A volley of shots rang out behind him, and as the rolling echoes died away, Dane clearly heard the clean shout from among the rocks at his back. The moonlight which had been their friend on the way up the mountain, was now their enemy, picking them out to their pursuers.

He heard the shrill whine of a slug cutting close to him, heard it spatter with a leaden hiss on the rock. Jerking himself instinctively back from the rock face, he ducked low in reflex instinct, ran along the winding trail. At every moment he expected to hear the sharp bark of another rifle and feel the leaden impact of a slug in his back, tearing through flesh and bone, seeking his heart. But he managed to reach the horses without that happening. The other was already in the saddle, waiting for him, holding the reins of his horse. Thrusting the Colts back into their holsters, he pulled himself up into the saddle, urged his mount forward, following the other. They descended as quickly as they dared, their horses careful of their footing, knowing that one false move could send them pitching to their deaths in the canyon, hundreds of feet below, at the bottom of that sheer drop. The air was cold, but the sweat came out under his hat band and made his forehead feel greasy. He had the trapped feeling for the first time in his life. Maybe he ought not to have listened to the old man in the first place when he had offered to lead him up here to the outlaw's hideout. But he had ridden into this with his eyes wide open and there was nobody to blame but himself. He cursed softly under his breath as he rode, feeling the horse slide dangerously under him as it fought to hold its footing on the slippery, treacherous rocks. A misstep could be just as fatal as a pause here. Already, those men would be moving in on them from behind, might even know a way over the rocks so as to be able to cut them off before they reached the point where the trail widened out at the base of the rocks, among the foothills.

They rode around a wide, sweeping bend in the trail. Here it widened out a little, there was more room in which to guide the horses without running the risk of going over the edge and Dane was bending low in the saddle to ease his own mount up close to the other's when the smashing explosion of a carbine, somewhere in the rocks on his right, made him flop forward in the saddle, holding himself low. He heard someone cry out above the sound of the rifle and a second later, the man in front of him threw up his arms and toppled from the saddle, hit the trail beside his loosely-running horse. Then his body spun to one side as a flailing hoof caught it and a second later, it was gone, over the side of the precipice and down into the black depths of the canyon.

Savagely, Dane jerked on the reins, pulling his mount to a sliding stop. Rocks bounced down the slope as the horse reared. Then Dane had dropped from the saddle, hitting the ground hard, pulling the horse into the side of the trail with one hand, gripping the

Colt in the other, swinging round to face the direction from which that shot had come, straining his eyes to try to pick out the location of the bush-whacker. The tantalizing tip of a rocky pinnacle showed less than fifty yards away, set in the darker, more confused mass of rock. It looked the most likely place a man would choose if he meant to shoot down a man on the trail, but Dane could not be sure the man he sought was there; and all the time, the precious seconds were ticking by, bringing the outlaws who must surely be on the trail at his back by now, closer to him. Soon, they would have hemmed him in and there would be no way by which he could escape. He probed the moonlit darkness of the trail in front of him. There was no sign of the oldster's horse and he guessed it would keep on running downtrail until it either went over the side or reached the bottom safely and headed back to town.

He cursed in a grating tone, pushed his body closer to the solid face of the cliff, risked a quick look around one of the tall boulders. The rifle barked again and he flinched as a clip of rock was smashed from the boulder and he felt the sting of powdered dust on his face and heard the vicious whine of the bullet as it ricocheted away into the darkness close to his shoulder. But that quick glance had been enough to tell him where the bushwhacker was hidden. Sweat popped out on his forehead and began to trickle into his eyes. He wiped it away with his free hand, blinked several times. He couldn't stay where he was and for the moment he was afraid to swing up into the saddle again and try to run that narrow trail where it ran across open ground and left him wide open to that hidden killer among the rocks.

There was no doubt that the bushwhacker knew all the tricks. He was keeping his head well down and fanning away the smoke from the rifle so that it was not easy to pick out his hiding place. Only the brief orange muzzle flash had given him away. Carefully, Dane lifted the Colt and sighted it on the rocks where he knew the other to be. Behind him, in the distance, but coming closer, he heard the yelling of the other men, as they worked their way along the narrow trail. The sense of time urging him to a decision was strong within him, swamping all other feelings.

The ground ahead was not conducive to fast flight and he knew that he would have to be off his mark very soon if he was to stand any chance of keeping ahead of these killers. A third shot boomed out, broke his reverie, made him jerk his head back out of sight. Almost before the echoes of the shot had died away, he sent a couple of slugs whistling into the rocks in the near distance. Neither of them found their mark and he forced himself to wait patiently with the gun sighted on the spot where he knew the dry-gulcher to be. A slight movement in the shadows. Then he saw the tall hat show above the rocks. He continued to wait, his finger hard on the trigger, his teeth clenched tightly in his head, trying not to think of the outlaws working their way nearer to him along the trail.

The pale blur of the man's head showed a second later as the other pushed himself up to get a better aim. Gently, Dane squeezed the trigger, felt the gun back in his wrist. The face vanished and he heard the harsh yell, knew that this time the slug had found its target. Without pausing to find out whether the other was dead or had only been wounded, he made a leap for the horse standing by the side of the trail, leapt up into the saddle and urged it forward, raking his spurs along its flanks. He felt sorry at the way he treated his mount, but there was now the pressing need to get down off the mountain trail as quickly as possible and he did not know just how long he had. The outlaws would not have been standing still after he had shot their lookout. They would have to hunt him down and kill him now that he knew just where their hide-out was located. That had probably been one of them up there in the rocks, possibly one of the other lookouts, alerted and alarmed by the shooting.

He veered along the trail, urging his mount to its fastest speed, legs and arms scraping the rough rock. Putting his horse across a narrow stretch of open ground he immediately heard the renewal of gunfire. The right hand wall of the canyon remained sheer as far as he could see and glancing back, he saw one of the men come into sight above the rocks, stand straight and tall, the rifle pressed into his shoulder to get an accurate aim. The bullet struck the rock less than six inches from him, scattering the flinty gravel as it ricocheted away into the night. He put the horse across the open ground, keeping low in the saddle, then paused for a few moments, studying the situation around him. The canyon now made a long slow turn downward into darker country where the moonlight was blotted out by the looming bulk of the mountain itself.

The slope twisted and wound in front of him; it was a rough slope, but a passable one even in the moonlight, once he crossed the twenty-yard stretch of tumbled boulders and sharp-edged flinty rocks, The horse stumbled slightly, fought to regain its balance, came to a full pause and moved on again, working its way forward. Gaining the temporary shelter of the pines which grew along the far slope, he stopped and swung about, his head moved slowly from side to side so that his eyes, held still, could concentrate on all the places as his head moved past. But he saw nothing. Either the outlaw gang had pulled back, or they were working their way past him, hoping to reach the bottom of the mountain trail before he did, cutting him off. Once he hit the plain down there, he felt certain that, even with a tired mount, he could outdistance his pursuers. But there was still a way to go and all the time, those men at his back might be moving forward through the rocks along the trails he did not even know existed.

He fought his way over some of the roughest country he had ever known. At every moment he expected his mount to stumble, break a leg, and leave him high and dry unable to get down off the mountain; but somehow, he kept its balance, picking its way cautiously down the trail. This was the way of it for half an hour. He heard no more gunfire behind him, but instead of allaying his fears, the silence only served to increase the feeling of apprehension that knotted the muscles of his stomach, bunching them into a hard ball, like a stone in the middle of his belly. Once, he was forced to dismount and lead his horse slowly forward as the trail narrowed. He did not recall riding along this particular stretch on the way up and fear hit him again, forcibly, as the possibility came to him that he might have lost his way somewhere along the downgrade trail and now he was lost in these hills. Presently, some kind of natural chute showed in the rocks, a wide wrinkle in the ground which would let him down gently on to the wider ledge some fifty feet below and from there, it was possible to see where the track opened out appreciably, with the smooth, dark shadow of the plain at the end of it. He took the chute and made better time once he reached the bottom. Heading east now, he thought he picked up the faint sound of a shout from the dark, shadowed rocks at his back; but it was impossible to be sure with the wind still keening shrilly in his ears. The trail wound in and out of tall walls of smoothly etched rock and turning the corner formed by one of these, he found himself on a gravel track that led straight down on to the prairie. Drawing a deep breath into his lungs, he exhaled slowly, wiping the sweat that had formed on his forehead, with the back of his hand.

The silence was charged with deadliness. Those men they had disturbed would not allow him to get back into town alive if they could help it. When a wisp of movement showed off to his right, Dane spotted it instantly, swung round. The tight bunch of riders had ridden down from a steep gully less than half a mile from the spot where he had come down from the foothills. That he had been seen was instantly obvious as a couple of shots rang out. The sound went splashing out over the plain with weakening echoes and a man's voice came loudly into the wake of the shots.

Screwing up his forehead as he tried to make out any other riders, converging on him from another direction, Dane put his horse towards the east, riding recklessly. He had waited too long after reaching the plain. The others had broken cover from a point where he had not expected them, were travelling diagonally over the smooth ground and would cut him off before he could reach the town.

Dane had a half mile lead on the men at his back. He heard the sound of their pursuit come steadily behind and at the end of a fifteen minute run he knew that they had decreased his lead appreciably. Usually one horse and one man made better time than a crowd, but this time, his own mount was tired, whereas theirs were fresh. He knew little of this land, yet for the moment he felt no concern about that. He was used to the open stretches of country from his boyhood, knew the pattern of hills and desert, of silence, heat and cold. He came presently on the stage trail, thundered along it, occasionally giving a quick glance over his shoulder at the bunch of men behind him. Almost a quarter of a mile separated them now and a few of their shots were coming dangerously close.

This was a new trail, travelled frequently by the coach and the freight wagons and he should have made excellent time, but his horse was tiring rapidly now and he knew he would have to turn and fight long before he reached town.

A shot boomed unexpectedly near and the dirt flew up less than six feet to one side of the horse. With a sudden start, he flung up his head, glanced back, then dropped his head again, crouched low in the saddle to present a more difficult target and gave his mount its head. The next shot came from a slightly different direction and now he knew that the men at his back were spreading out, coming in at him in a wide semi-circle; no longer tightly bunched.

Narrowing his eyes, Dane glanced ahead, peering into the darkness. Just at the limit of his vision, he made out the steep-sided canyon that lifted on either side of the trail, where it narrowed swiftly. He remembered this point from the previous ride, knew it was the only place where he stood a chance of holding off these killers at his back A quick glance behind him confirmed that they were now beginning to swing in, confident that they had him trapped. Gritting his teeth, he eased his tight-fisted hold on the reins.

The sound of shots grew and came down to him on the wind which flowed from his back. Then he was in the narrow notch of the canyon, the high, rough walls of rock holding him strictly to the trail. There was less than half a mile of this, he remembered, before he came out into open ground again, and it would be difficult, if not impossible, for the riders to move around it. The rocks stretched away for a long way in either direction and the trail was the only road through. The firing remained brisk even though he was now out of sight of the outlaws. Then he heard the firing die away into a silence made ringingly hollow by the din of the racket that had gone just before. Halfway along the canyon, he halted his mount, slid from the saddle and ran for the shelter of a rocky ledge. He was still trapped in the canyon, but here the trail was so narrow that it was impossible for more than two men to ride abreast. Tugging the Colts from their holsters, he crouched there in the cold darkness and waited tensely, peering into the back channel of the trail, glancing anxiously at the shadowed banks of rock that lifted steeply from the sides of the trail. Someone in the distance shouted, the yell carrying above the pounding of hoofbeats on the rocky floor of the canyon. The column of men was almost dead on him, slackening speed now, obviously wary of a trap.

Dane smiled thinly as he lifted the guns, sighting on the dark mass of shadow that came along the trail. The men were jostling themselves a little as they rode forward and he let them come within twenty feet before thumbing back the hammers of the Colts and letting them both go in the same instant. Dane watched one of the shadows waver and fall away as the man slipped from the saddle. He heard him strike ground and grunt. The column hauled up instantly as men found themselves boxed in by the walls of the canyon, as men and horses choked this narrow way, swaying in confused motion, men riding back and forth restlessly, trying to find cover before more slugs roared among them.

Dane loosed off another couple of shots, heard a man yell out with a loud, agonized bleat of sound, knew that another bullet had found its mark. The men recovered their composure quickly. Another shout and they were scattering for the rocks, crouching down. He saw the brief orange muzzle flashes as they fired wildly into the darkness, trying to pick out where he was. The sound of bullets striking wide of his position made him smile a little. Gently, he eased his way back among the jumbled rocks, picking his way cautiously, placing his feet carefully so as not to dislodge none of the loose boulders.

The volley of fire grew in intensity and now, as more and more slugs hummed like a swarm of angry hornets through the darkness, some of them were coming dangerously close to where he lay. Sooner or later, they would smother this area with gunfire, and under cover of it, some of them would move forward; already he knew there were several crouched down on this side of the trail and it was only a matter of time before they began to move forward. He cast about him with anxious eyes, probing the darkness that lay behind him, trying to find a way out of this portion of the trail without exposing himself to the outlaws' fire.

Narrowing his eyes, he made out the two dark figures that suddenly darted across the open stretch of the trail and vanished into the shadows on his own side of the track before he could get in a shot at them. He heard the scrape of their boots on the smooth rocks as they edged their way slowly forward, knew that the rest of the men were only waiting for him to risk a shot at them and the muzzle flash from his gun would give him away at once.

A sharp volley of shots cracked out a second later, and almost before the echoes had died away there was a savage, and totally unexpected, reply from the rocks just behind him and a little above where he lay. Swiftly, he flung a backward glance in the direction of that single gunshot, but he could see nothing for several seconds, then a dark figure wormed its way down the narrow trail and moved down beside him. The girl held the rifle tightly in her hands, looked at him for a moment in the darkness.

'I thought it had to be you,' she said in a harsh whisper. 'Nobody else would be foolish enough to try to take on this bunch unaided. How did you manage to find them — or is that a stupid question?' She punctuated her remark with a quick shot along the trail and out of the corner of his eye, Dane saw a man leap up suddenly, throw his hands up in front of his face, then fall back on to the trail.

'I didn't take 'em on unaided,' he

retorted through clenched teeth. 'I had a guide who promised to lead me to their hideout.'

'It certainly looks as though he succeeded,' muttered the girl. 'And where is he now? Did he ride on back into town when he saw what had happened, leaving you to face these men alone?'

'One of their look-outs spotted us in the moonlight. He was silenced but the others moved in after us. They shot the old man who'd taken me up yonder.'

The girl looked at him sharply. There was an expression on her face he could not quite see, could not define. 'Old Jeb Crossman,' she said tightly. 'It must have been him. He's the only one in town who might have had an idea where this bunch hide out. You say he's dead?'

'Afraid so. He went over the edge of the trail after they'd shot him.'

The girl gave him a stone-still glance, then jerked her head in the direction of the outlaw bunch. 'We can't stand them off for long,' she murmured. 'We'll have to make a break for it pretty soon. Your horse is along the trail a piece. I spotted him a moment ago.'

Scarcely had she finished speaking, when a man's voice came from the tumble of rocks on the far side of the trail. It was hard to place it exactly.

'Hey! You in there! Come on out or we'll fetch you out.'

Dane frowned, trying to place the voice. He couldn't. The echoes, rattling along the trail and among the tall, sky-rearing rocks, made it impossible to estimate where the man was exactly and he did not dare risk another blind shot.

'Why don't you come on in and get me?' he called back.

'We'll do just that,' called the voice once more. 'When we do, we'll kill you. Your only chance is to come on out right now.'

'Now what kind of a fool do you reckon I am,' Dane hollered back. He turned and looked at the girl. Her eyes shone in the shadow of her face with a dark intensity. 'We may be able to work our way back along the trail I came along,' she said softly. 'If we try to make a break for it along the main trail, they'll nail us before we make it to the horses.'

Dane threw a quick glance behind him at the towering mass of rock, then nodded in agreement. it was the only chance they had of getting out of there alive and slim as it was, they had to take it. 'Let's move,' he said tautly.

Edging back, he followed the girl among the rocks, flattening his body against the tall boulders whenever any shots from the hidden men came close. The outlaws were still firing blind, there seemed little doubt about that. Equally doubtlessly they were beginning to close in under cover of rifle fire.

The trail here was narrower and rougher than any part of that which he had climbed and descended in the mountains earlier that night and as they reached the topmost point, where it moved around a wide outcrop of rock,

Dane saw to his dismay that the first faint grey flush of dawn was already beginning to show low in the east. Soon it would be light enough for the men at his back to spot them and then they would be finished. A slug tore a sliver of rock away from the edge of the trail immediately behind them, almost on Dane's heels. Savagely, he forced down the rising sense of panic, made himself move on after the girl, picking her way carefully over the loose rocks which lay strewn over the trail. Now they were around the bulging outcrop of rock, out of sight of the men at their back. They could still hear sporadic firing and Dane guessed that the men were moving in slowly, not sure of where he was.

Down below him, he saw the shapes of two horses, one his own and the other evidently belonging to the girl. He dropped lightly on to the trail, held out his hand to help the girl; then they took the reins and walked the horses along the trail for a little way before mounting up and riding on into the faint light of an early dawn.

'I reckon that's the second time you've stepped in and saved my life,' Dane said harshly, when they were well away from the canyon, out in open country. 'I figured you'd be on your way home by now.'

'I got back to the house before midnight,' said the girl, and there was a strange note in her voice. 'Someone had managed to get through the cordon of men my father keeps around the place. They had taken a shot at him through the window of the room. I was riding into town to get the doctor when I heard the sound of gunfire and rode over to investigate.'

'Lucky for me that you did,' Dane stopped suddenly, stiffening. 'You say that somebody shot your father.'

'That's right. I don't know how bad the wound is. He was still conscious when I left him and two of the men are with him now, doing what they can for him, but I'm sure the bullet is still inside him.'

'I'll ride back with you once you've got the doctor, if I may,' said Dane. 'There's something goin' on around these parts that I sure don't understand. I reckon maybe your father might be able to help me. If he's too ill to talk, of course, then I won't try to question him.'

The girl's face was a mask. Already, the dawn was spreading over the eastern half of the sky and the stars and moon had begun to dim. He threw an anxious look over his shoulder but there was no sign of his pursuers.

As if divining his thoughts, Victoria Maller said quietly, confidently: 'You don't need to worry about those men now. We're too close to town for them to hunt us any further. But you'll know better than to go into the hills again, particularly along that trail.'

'I hope you're right. I don't particularly want to tangle with them until I'm good and ready. I can see it was a mistake to go into the hills last night.'

'You any idea who you were looking for?' queried the girl archly.

Dane nodded. 'Clem Keeler,' he said shortly.

'Then you know that he's leading those outlaws,' The girl spoke slowly and quietly.

'Yes, I knew that,' Dane nodded shortly. 'Just as surely as I know that when I next meet him face to face, I'm goin' to kill him. I've got a score to settle with him and I want him to know who it is who's pullin' the trigger that sends him into eternity.'

'You must hate him very much,' said the girl softly.

Dane nodded, but said nothing. Half an hour later, with the grey in the east turning swiftly to a brilliant red-yellow, they rode into El Amaro, walked their mounts along the main street and paused in front of the doctor's place. The girl dismounted quickly and went inside, while Dane sat his saddle, rolling himself a cigarette. The smoke helped to ease the tenson in him, relaxed the taut muscles a little.

Presently, the door opened and the girl reappeared, the tall figure of the black-coated doctor behind her. The other glanced up at him, then a curious gust of expression passed over his thin, pinched features.

'You're the man who shot up those two Bar W riders, ain't you?' he gritted.

'That's right,' Dane told him. 'But I reckon we'd better hurry.'

The other paused, then unhitched the horse from the rail, pulled himself slowly into the saddle, swung his mount's head towards the end of the street and fell into step beside Dane and the girl. Out of town, they took the trail that led south, into the land of contrasts, over the narrow, wooden bridge and through the short stretch of rocky ground on the far bank of the river, before they began to climb. In the distance, low hills lay before them, purple and red with the first rays of the sun where it touched the tall peaks and yet left the valleys in deep shadow. The cold of the night air was still around them, seeping through Dane's clothing and into his bones, but gradually, it was lessening in its intensity and he knew that within an hour, the sun would be up and the heat of the day would begin. He eyed the hills and trees around the trail. His glance was quick-moving but not restless; confident and poised in its own way, unafraid and now totally without emotion of any kind. It hadn't come to be like that naturally. There had been long years down in the Badlands, along the frontier, where a man had to be quick on the trigger and to be unwary was to be dead.

Since Clem Keeler had set the law on him, had turned him into a hunted man, an awful resentment and thirst for vengeance had blossomed in him, and he had been forced into the environment which peels and strips away all those things that make life good for a man. Now he had two things — perfect confidence and perfect co-ordination, the two things which every gunfighter had to have and could not exist without.

They swung down the wide trail, over the crest of a long, bony ridge and then down into the wide valley which lay spread out before them in the pearly light of morning. It looked lush and peaceful down there, thought Dane to himself; and it was hard to realize that any moment now, a full-scale range war might flare up and cover this land with the heavy stench of gunpowder. He had seen it happen before and was well aware of the consequences of this, knew that nobody really came out of such a gunfight the victor.

Men came out of the house, eyed Dane and the doctor curiously, but made no comment as they rode into the small courtyard beside the corral, unsaddled and turned their mounts loose. Two men stood on the porch as they went inside; tall, hard-faced men, their features etched with shadow as the sun began to lift clear of the looming bulk of the hill in the distance. Inside the house, Dane followed the girl along the narrow passage and into the room at the back of the house. The man he had earlier rescued from Skinner and his bunch lay on the bed in one corner, the sheets pulled up to his chin. His face bore a whitish pallor now under the tan. There was a crude bandage over his shoulder and around his chest and his breathing was harsh and sharp, although he was quite conscious, one hand upstretched, fingers gripping the iron post of the bed, knuckles standing out white and taut under the skin.

Dane closed the bedroom door, stood against it while the doctor went forward and stood beside the bed, looking down. Sweat lay on the settler's forehead, beaded here and there with a little of it trickling down on to his cheeks.

'What happened here?' asked the doctor harshly. It was evident that he had no great liking for nesters, but now that this man was a patient for him, he was clearly resigned to looking upon him as such.

'Gunshot,' muttered the other. 'Through the window yonder.' He tried to lift his head but the effort proved too much for him and he sank back on to the pillow. Dane glanced round, saw where the glass of the window had been splintered by the bullet.

Gently, the doctor unwound the bandages around Maller's chest, probed the wound in his shoulder with deft fingers. He nodded as if to himself: 'Looks like it shaved a rib — or maybe broke one. The slug's still there. I'll have to dig for it.' He sighed, turned to the girl. 'If you've got any whiskey in the house, better bring it. I can use it as a disinfectant and I think your father will need some to dull the pain.'

Victoria went out of the room and the doctor rose to his feet, pulling off his coat and rolling up the sleeves of his shirt. He turned his glance to Dane. 'You can help too, mister,' he said quietly. 'I'll need someone to help hold him down. It's goin' to be rough on him when I get started.'

Dane nodded and moved forward. In his time, he had been forced to do a little crude surgery himself. When a man rode a lonely trail, there were times when he came face to face with a situation like this; and he soon learned how to set a busted arm or leg, or dig out a bullet from a shoulder or leg. If infection got into such a wound and the man died, then that was just too bad. The men out here had to be tough or they went by the board.

'You this man's friend?' grunted the doctor.

'Let's say I stopped a bunch of cattlemen from hangin' him,' Dane said. He looked at the other close and careful. 'Whether these settlers, these homesteaders are doin' a good job or not bein' in this territory, I don't know. Their personal quarrel with the cattle bosses is no quarrel of mine.'

'If you stick by them, then it's your quarrel whether you like it or not,' affirmed the other harshly. He glanced round as Victoria came into the room with the whiskey and a bowl of boiling water, setting them both on the small table beside the bed.

Maller tried to grin away the hurt of his injury as Dane gripped him by the good arm, but sweat lay beaded on his forehead and upper lip and the growing warmth in the house showed on his flushed features now.

'You got any idea who did this?' Dane asked tightly, as the doctor prepared his instruments.

Weakly, Maller shook his head. 'Must've been one of the Skinner crew,' he muttered thickly. 'Unless one of them outlaws from the hills decided to do this.'

'Wasn't any of them,' said Dane decisively. 'They were too busy tryin' to kill me through the night to do this job.'

Maller's eyes widened just a shade at that, but he made no comment. Victoria filled a glass with the raw whiskey, stood over him, supporting the glass while her father gulped it down. Liquor spilled down the front of his chest and he squirmed on the bed, coughing and spluttering a little as the raw liquid bit the back of his throat. He tried to smile, but there was no mirth in it.

4

Range War

Gently, the doctor probed inside the raw-looking wound for the piece of lead that had been the cause of all this trouble. A faint film of sweat on his forehead testified to the concentration of him as he pressed his lips tightly together, occasionally pausing to wipe the sweat away and to clean his hands where the perspiration formed a greasy layer on the palms, making it difficult for him to hold the instrument properly. He sucked in a sharp breath, said thinly through his teeth.

'Reckon it must've touched the shoulder blade and gone in deeper than I figured.' He sat back, stared down at the man on the bed for a long moment, then looked up at Dane. 'No need to keep a hold on him now, young fella.

He's passed out cold. Maybe it's better that way. At least, he won't feel anythin' until I'm through.' He forced a quick grin. 'Never really did believe in whiskey to dull a man's pain. His grief, maybe, but not somethin' like this.'

Bending forward, flexing the long, tapered fingers a little he went back to work, forehead creased, brows drawn together in a hard, straight line. Dane watched closely, acutely aware of the girl standing in the background, unobtrusive and quiet, while the doctor fought for her father's life.

Presently, a long sigh came from the doctor's lips and he straightened up, something small and ugly held in the metal jaws of the forceps. He dropped it on to the polished top of the table where it made a dull, metallic sound. 'That's it,' he said softly. 'Now all we can do is bind up the wound and let his constitution do the rest. He's a pretty strong man and I reckon he ought to pull through. But he'll be in bed for two or three weeks and no excitement.' His glance lifted to the girl. 'You got any men who can work this place while he's in bed?'

The girl nodded her head slowly. 'We've got the men,' she said slowly.

'Good.' The doctor got to his feet, began to replace the instruments in his bag. He was silent for a moment, then said: 'You want me to tell the Sheriff about this shootin' when I get back to town?' The way in which he said it, made it clear that he knew the answer he would get before the girl spoke.

Victoria looked at him strangely for a moment, lips pressed together in an almost wilful line. Then she gave a hard smile and there was a curious brightness in her eyes. 'Do you think that would make any difference, doctor; as far as the law is concerned? In this part of the territory, anybody can shoot a settler and the law will take no action. Sheriff Keeler is only sheriff so long as Ed Skinner and the other cattlemen say so. We all know that.'

The doctor rubbed his chin thoughtfully, then his gaze fell away a little. 'I guess you're right.' He moved over to the door. 'Let him rest today. Tomorrow you can start feeding him somethin' nourishin'.'

When the doctor had gone, Dane went out on to the porch. The air was cool and clear, but with the sun just glinting through the bunch of trees on top of the tall hill to the south-east of the house. The small herd had moved out from its sleeping quarters and was grazing in the middle of the stretching patch of grassland. He leaned himself against one of the uprights, took paper and tobacco from his pocket and rolled a smoke. From the porch, he got a good picture of the land here. It looked good. A man could spend most of his days in a place such as this if he was left alone to enjoy them, he thought wearily. But good country that it was, there was the feeling deep inside him that all hell was due to be let loose at any moment now. With the shooting of Maller like this, he felt sure that the torch had been set to the powder train which would spark off a range war. The nester had been so sure when he had last seen him that nobody could get through the cordon of men with which he had surrounded himself, and harm him. Now, it seemed, he had been wrong and a mistake like that had almost cost hint his life.

There was a soft movement at his back and he turned to find the girl standing there, watching him speculatively. She sat down in the shadows of the porch and her voice dropped low. 'He thought he was safe here, that nobody could get into the yard and take a shot at him.'

'Somebody got in,' Dane told her seriously.

She nodded, remained silent over a long period, sitting there with her hands on her knees, body bent forward a little, looking out into the sunlight, her face sober and indrawn. When she spoke again, there was a fresh note in her voice. 'I can see that there's going to be nothing but trouble here. The cattlemen are determined to run us out of the territory and there's nothing we can do to stop them.'

'Won't the Government help?' asked Dane.

'We sent someone to Virginia City to try to get help, but they merely said that the land was ours, that our title deeds would be recognized in law and that they could only spare troops if any fighting broke out on a large scale. It seems that they mean to wait until a lot of blood has been shed before they take any action. Sometimes, I get to thinking that maybe we ought not to stay here and risk our lives, that even the Government is working with the cattlemen, although they do their best not to show it, or admit it — except by doing nothing when we ask for help.'

'How many settlers are there here, in this valley?'

She shrugged. 'Thirty, forty perhaps. Not many more.'

'And the cattlemen can call on a hundred men if they need to,' mused Dane softly. He lifted his head and stared off into the hills that lay blue and tall on the horizon. 'This is a country worth fighting for,' he said at length.

The girl suddenly hit him with her suppressed irritation. 'Why should we have to fight for it?' she demanded harshly. She got to her feet and paced nervously back and forth along the porch. 'Surely there's room for everyone out here. We only take the land which has been given to us. We don't ask for the prairies as these other people seem to think.'

Dane ceased to smile. 'They'll never compromise with you,' he said soberly. 'They'll fight you to the end. And even if you do beat them, those outlaws in the hills are just waitin' for the chance to ride down and take everythin'.'

'We know.' The girl stroked her long, shoulder-length hair with her fingers and there was a certain wistfulness in her look. 'This land is rough, but we have to come here and try to make a life for ourselves, sink our roots deep, because if we don't this country is never going to be great.'

Dane glanced at her in surprise. She had far more vision than he had credited her with, could see further than most men he had known. Then he nodded. 'You'll have to get your men, bring in every one who can handle a gun and force a showdown with the cattlemen and their trail crews. Fight for this place against them.'

'Do you really think that we have a chance?' There was a trace of scorn in her voice. 'Go up against Ed Skinner and the others and we would be finished. Besides, there aren't many of us who can handle a gun like the professional killers they've hired to protect their ranches.'

'I know. But if you don't, then they'll come and destroy you. They'll attack you one by one, when you least expect them and if you're divided, as you are now, they'll take you without any trouble. Hasn't the fact that somebody managed to get to your father shown you that you're not safe from them, even when you're on your own land?'

'What do you think I should do?' For a moment, her voice sounded pathetic, crying for help, unsure of herself.

'Get a couple of your men to ride out to the other homesteads, get all of the men together — bring them here, because unless I miss my guess, this is where Skinner means to attack. He hates your father even more than he fears what he's doin'. Now that he knows he can walk in here any time and shoot down a man in his own house, he'll waste no time getting his hellions together and ridin' against you. Besides, he knows he'll have to do it before your father is on his feet again; he knows that your father is the one rallying point in this territory for the other homesteaders.'

'I'll try.' Victoria stared at him; revealing nothing of her thoughts. 'But it won't be easy. They're afraid, all of them.'

'Can't blame 'em,' nodded Dane slowly. He thought to himself: *Some of them are going to get themselves killed before long, and nobody wants it to be him.*

★   ★   ★

Dane reached his horse, led it out of the wide corral, climbed into the saddle and made a slow circuit of the homestead, aware that the girl was watching him with curious eyes from the shadow of the porch. Reining the bay in front of her, he said: 'Just figured I'd take a look around Skinner's place. Might as well see what sort of opposition you've got — and I may be able to spot 'em if they are gatherin' there, ready to move out.'

'What about the man you came to kill?' The girl spoke quietly and dispassionately, as if it were the most natural thing in the world that a man would want to hunt down another human being and kill him without compunction.

'There'll come a time for that,' he murmured harshly. 'In the meantime, be ready to collect all the men you can together.'

She nodded her head and he saw hurt in her eyes, but strangely, there was no fear in them now. It was as if she had suddenly resigned herself to things as they were, had realized that she could not change the frontier ways of violence and that if she was to remain here, it was something with which she would have to live.

Touching spurs to the bay, he rode out of the dusty courtyard, took the trail that wound up over the side of the hill. Cattle moved bawling out of his way and he noticed the small group of men, sitting their mounts in the near distance. They looked efficient and useful men. If they could be trusted to stand their ground when the showdown came, they would fight well. He sincerely hoped that they would stick by the girl and her wounded father, and not ride on over the hill once the going proved to be tougher than they had bargained for.

As he rode, he thought over in his mind all that he knew about Keeler, the reputed leader of these outlaws, the son of the sheriff of El Amaro. If the other kept his finger on things happening in the territory, then let him think that all he was doing was helping these nesters against the cattle barons. Keeler was brilliant, utterly evil and sly. He had to be, to run this outlaw band and still keep that knowledge both from his father and most of the townsfolk in El Amaro. But the fact that some people there had already guessed at his identity, showed that he was not quite as clever as he imagined himself to be. Instinctive anger flooded over him and he gripped the reins more tightly than was necessary, the muscles of his jaw lumped under the skin.

He climbed a rising hogback of

ground, moved through a small grove of trees, then found himself on an open, scree-covered stretch of ground that jutted out over the wide valley which lay before him. He could feel as well as see the immensity of the country here. It all lay in front of him, a limitless ocean of ground, moving out to the horizons as far as the eye could see. The deep and brooding agelessness of the country touched him deeply. Swinging round, he rode north, along the switchback courses, crossed a narrow stream which came bubbling swiftly in a rush of white-touched foam from the top of the hills. He felt the swift rush of water clutch at the horse's legs and it staggered briefly for a moment, then regained its balance and moved slowly forward, picking its way carefully over the smoothly rounded stones of the stream bed.

The sun lay hot and heavy on his back and shoulders and his shadow was small now that it had almost reached its zenith, sending waves of heat back from the yellow rocks on either side of the trail. The heat head was a heavy and oppressive pressure, like the flat of a mighty hand pressing into the ground, stifling him with every breath he drew into his lungs. Cutting down towards the lower slopes, he soon came to a point where he could look down and see over the whole of the rangeland. The high rise of ground gave him a good, clear picture of the full extent of the Skinner spread. He had heard that the place was big, but he had not realized that it was as big as this. Far off, in the blue-hazed distance, he could make out the ranch itself, barns and corrals set around the central house, with the bunkhouses to one side.

Nearer at hand, a wide valley opened out on to the range itself where the cattle were and the mountain stream which he had forded a little while earlier ran through the valley and twin ditches stole the water which over-flowed from it and carried it out to a large patch of green. The ranch road twisted and wound through the valley and then on and away into the distance to where he could no longer see it.

Slipping from the saddle, Dane eyed the scene, for a long moment while he rolled himself a smoke. From his vantage point, he could see all there was to see without being seen himself from down below. Small wonder that Skinner wanted the valley which had been taken over by Maller. The other nesters, he reckoned, would have the land which bordered on the rangeland to the south and east. Now, they would hem in the big cattle outfits and men like Skinner might be looking ahead to a time when they could foresee the range itself all neatly parcelled up into smaller squares of land, taken over by the home-steaders, with barbed wire up all across the country, strung so that there would be no free passage of the vast cattle herd across the state.

Presently, when he had finished his smoke, he moved back into the shade of the trees. The heat head had increased in its piled-up intensity and was now a stifling, choking pressure which made it difficult to breath, and the air felt as if it had been drawn over a vast oven before reaching him.

In spite of himself, his head nodded forward on to his chest and he dozed off, the heat of the sun making it impossible for him to keep his eyes open. When he finally woke, he saw by the shadow of the trees, that he had slept for some hours and he cursed himself for succumbing to the weariness in his body. Anything might have happened down there while he had been asleep. Stiffly, he got to his feet and stared down into the valley, narrowing his eyes against the flooding light of the slowly sinking sun. The next minute, he was crawling forward to the very edge of the rising hump of ground, keeping his head low, peering down in the direction of the ranch. There was plenty of activity down there now, he noticed. The herd which earlier had been out on the grassland in the distance, had been brought closer to the ranch and there were more than two score of horses in the corral, with others hitched to the post outside the porch of the ranch. Men lounged around the courtyard, obviously waiting for some order to be given and he could guess at what that order might be. The sight of those men down there was a signal of things to come and he thought of Victoria Maller, back at the homestead with a badly wounded father and only a mere handful of men to back her up if these gunmen were given the order to ride against them. The thought of that evoked a hard sense of anger in him. Even as he watched, another bunch of men came spurring their mounts along the narrow ranch road, dismounted in front of the lowroofed house and went inside, leaving their mounts hitched to the rail. Evidently the gunhawks were receiving their orders to be ready to ride out and destroy.

'You lookin' for something?'

Swiftly, Dane swung round, cursing

himself for not having realized that there was the trail to his back along which he had ridden at high noon. Three riders were sitting their mounts, staring down at him. One had caught hold of his own bay and was holding the reins in his hand. He was a thin-faced, cadaverous looking man, his flesh white under the tan, drawn down tightly on his cheek bones. Only his black eyes burned under the bushy brows. The other men were broad, square, massively built, one wearing a bedraggled black beard which accentuated the sallowness of his skin.

'Ain't no law against lookin', is there?' Dane growled. He tightened his lips to hide the deepseated anger he felt within him at having been taken off guard like this. There was no doubting that these were three of Skinner's crew, all carrying guns slung low at their waists and with rifles thrust into the scabbards on their saddles.

'That all depends on what you're lookin' at,' grunted the thin-faced man.

'Mister Skinner ain't particularly fond of folk sypin' on his land. Could be you're one of these rustlers who've been takin' the cattle off the north range, lookin' the place over again, ready for the next time.'

There was no chance for Dane to reach out for his mount and get away from these three men. He even doubted if he would be able to get the drop on all three of them, although the thought of such action lived in his eyes for a brief moment. One of the men must have noticed his guarded look, for his right hand moved quickly, down and up, and Dane saw the black hole of a Colt muzzle staring at him over the pommel of the other's saddle. The look on the man's face did not change at all as he said: 'I figure we ought to let Mister Skinner take a look at you, stranger. Then he can decide what to do with folk who come up here spyin' on his ranch. When we got here you seemed mighty interested in what was goin' on down there, so interested that you didn't even hear us approach.'

Dane clamped his teeth tightly together, said nothing. His mind was a whirling chaos of half-formed thoughts and ideas. The man cocked the gun in his fist, moved his horse a little to one side of the trail and motioned Dane forward. The barrel of the gun was still lined upon his chest and the hand which held it was rock steady. He did not doubt that the other would kill him instantly if he made a wrong move.

The cadaverous-looking man came forward, taking care not to get between his companion with the gun and Dane. Reaching down, he took the slender rope from around the saddlehorn, then dragged Dane's hands behind his back, tying the rope tightly around his wrists. Then he reached down and plucked the two Colts from his holsters and tossed them into the trees.

'All right, stranger,' he said tightly. 'Let's ride down to the ranch.'

They rode slowly, moving on either side of him, watchful and alert, not trusting him even though he was trussed up so that he could not possibly use his hands. Fortunately the ground was smooth and ten minutes after leaving the crest of the ridge, they hit the ranch trail and headed towards the cluster of buildings in the distance. Out of the corner of his eye, Dane noticed the sudden stiffening of the small groups of men around the courtyard when he and his captors rode in. There was an immediate heightening of tension. The thin-featured man caught the reins of his mount and hauled the bay to a standstill in front of the house.

'Get down,' he said harshly.

For an instant, Dane sat in the saddle. Then he managed to hook one leg over in front of him and dropped to the ground. Off-balance, unable to use his hands to steady himself, he fell forward into the sunbaked dust, felt it grind into his face, scouring his cheeks. A hoarse laughter lifted from the men near the porch. He sensed, rather than saw one of the squarely-built men come

156

forward, his foot drawn back. The toe of his boot caught Dane in the small of the back, pitched him forward again, lips pressed tightly together to stifle the yell of pain as red-edged agony burst through the lower half of his body. He rolled over, expecting another kick, hoping to miss it, but the other remained where he was, grinning viciously down at him, lips thinned back over his tobacco-stained teeth.

With an effort, he managed to get his feet under him, staggered upright, sucking in great gulps of air. His insides felt as if they had been caught and twisted by a red-hot knife and he knew the sweat was pouring down his face as he stood there, eyes narrowed.

The man caught him by the arm, thrust him forward roughly in the direction of the house. Stumbling up the wooden steps on to the porch, Dane somehow managed to keep his balance although his vision was oddly blurred. The muscles along the small of his back still ached and throbbed intolerably but he forced himself to ignore the pain as he went inside, the barrel of a Colt pushed hard into his spine.

'In here,' said the man at his back, motioning him towards the door at the end of the passage.

Dane went inside, looked about him quickly. Ed Skinner and several other men stood by the open window at the far side of the room.

'Caught this *hombre* on the edge of the south pasture, boss,' said his captor. 'Looked to us as if he was spyin' on the ranch. Anyways, he seemed mighty interested in what was goin' on down here.'

Skinner's glance held on Dane's like black iron. He grinned viciously. 'I guess this time your luck has run out, mister,' he muttered. 'Ain't nobody here to butt in this time.'

'If you're figuring on finishing me and then ridin' in to take the nesters at the Maller spread, you're in for a big surprise,' he said thinly, speaking through clenched teeth. 'You didn't think that you could send one of your men out there to shoot down old man Maller in cold blood and not rouse the whole lot of those homesteaders against you, did you, Skinner?'

'You tryin' to tell me that they have more men backing them than I have,' Skinner shook his head slowly, still grinning. 'If you are, then you're a bigger fool than I figured. You've seen the men I've got outside, and there are as many again, waiting for me to give the word to ride. No, my friend, the nesters are finished, just as you are.'

'I wouldn't be too sure of that,' Dane said. He attempted to force conviction into his voice.

'Yeah, we'll see about that. I intend to ride out to the Maller place tonight and there ain't nobody goin' to stop me. Not even if he manages to round up every nester in the territory.'

The rest of the men in the room were studying Dane closely. He did not recognize any of them as the men who had accompanied Skinner when he had tried to hang Maller. Then Skinner inhaled a big breath and let it out noisily. He chuckled softly. Turning to the men who had brought Dane in, he said: 'Bring Marty. I reckon he ought to be in on this.'

The other went out, closing the door behind him. Skinner grinned tightly. 'You don't know Marty,' he muttered. 'But you shot his brother yesterday mornin'. I promised him that he'd have you if we ever managed to run you to earth. Somehow, I doubt if he reckoned on getting even with you as soon as this.'

There was a movement behind Dane as the door opened once more. His captor stepped into the room and behind him was a little, wizened-faced man, his jet-black eyes darting questioningly towards Dane.

'Figured you two had better meet, Marty,' said Skinner. The look on his face told Dane that he was enjoying himself immensely, playing this cat and mouse game with him. 'This is the *hombre* who jumped us yesterday mornin' and shot down your brother and Bent Morgan.'

Dane saw the change come over the gunman's face, saw the way he looked at him with a peculiar, unfocused expression. 'What do you figure on doin' with him?'

'Now that's a good question,' Skinner's smile widened. 'I reckon it's only justice that I turn him over to you. I don't want him killed around the ranch, but I reckon you could take him for a little ride up into the hills. Make sure that he doesn't bother me any more; and as for yourself, get back here before dark. We ride at sundown.'

The black-blue eyes matched the nonchalant shrug which the gunman gave as he turned on Dane. The glance was eloquent enough as he grinned viciously. His right hand hovered dangerously close to the gun at his waist as he jerked a thumb in the direction of the door at his back. 'All right, killer,' he snapped crisply. 'Get outside and on to your horse. You and me are goin' to take a little ride like the boss says.' Dane guessed what the other had in mind, but he gave no sign of it.

Under the watchful eye of the hawk-faced gunman, Dane clambered up awkwardly into the saddle. The cattlemen had not loosened the thong around his wrists and another roar of hoarse laughter went up as he swayed precariously in the saddle, almost losing his balance. Marty called to one of the men and his own mount was brought over. Easily, he swung into the saddle, then motioned him forward, a brooding sullenness in his eyes and a dark unpleasantness on his features.

They rode out of the ranch and took the road towards the hills. The mid-down sun shone straight into their eyes and Dane lowered his head a little, hooking his legs under the belly of the bay as the trail got rough in places, making it difficult for him to keep his hold.

When the gunmen had searched him

earlier after surprising him on the hill, they had taken away his two guns, but he still had the knife thrust into his belt under the shirt. If only he could loosen the thongs which bound his wrists, he might get a chance to use the weapon. It was going to be the only chance he would get. Behind his back, he worked steadily at the ropes until his wrists were raw and bleeding, but in spite of the pain he forced himself to persevere. Marty rode beside him, eyes occasionally probing ahead, looking for a good spot along the trail where death might come quickly and there would be no eyes watching.

The man who had tied the knots in the ropes had known his job and his struggles seemed to have no effect on the thongs whatever. Out of the corner of his eyes, he saw the other watching him tautly. With an effort, he forced himself to relax. If the other once suspected what he was trying to do, he would shoot him down there and then, without mercy.

'This ain't goin' to be quick, cowboy,' grinned Marty. 'I'm goin' to make sure that you take your time dyin'. Weren't no love lost between me and my brother, but nobody shoots any kin o' mine and gets away with it.'

'Why don't you see sense,' muttered Dane harshly. 'Skinner is headin' into big trouble when he rides against those homesteaders and he knows it. Only he won't be riskin' his neck — you will. You and the others. Then you'll have those outlaws to fight because they'll move in the minute you've finished fighting.'

'You seem to know a lot, mister,' grated the other, 'but even if they do as you say, you won't be around to see it. I'm goin' to kill you.'

Dane tightened his lips, said nothing. Perhaps it was his imagination, or merely wishful thinking, but the ropes that bound his wrists together behind his back felt looser than before, as if his endless twisting and tensing had succeeded in easing off the knots which had bitten deep into his flesh. Striving to keep all expression from his face, he continued to work on them, forcing himself to ignore the pain that lanced through his hands and arms with every movement he made.

The other was glancing ahead of him now, to where the trail turned into a rocky strip of ground. There were clumps of thorn, mesquite and sour apple flourishing there in this poisonous ground where nothing good could live and thrive. The trail here wound along the edge of a narrow, but deep gully, still filled with midnight shadow. Dane tensed the muscles of his shoulders, felt a little thrill race through his body. This was where the other intended to finish him, he reflected. There was no doubt about that. Just as undoubtedly, as the fact that the ropes were now slipping from around his hands as he tugged on them. There was no chance for him to massage the chafed and bloodied flesh, or to get much of the feeling back into his fingers. The look on the gunman's face had hardened considerably now and Dane was able to see the light of growing action in his eyes.

Presently, Marty slowed the gait of his horse, turned in the saddle with a broad smile on his face, a smile that twisted his thin lips into an animal-like snarl but did not touch his eyes. They were as cold and empty and bleak as ever.

'Reckon this is as good a place as any, Averill,' he grated thickly. 'We don't want to leave any evidence around for folks to find.' He glanced up meaningly at the blue mirror of the sky overhead. Dane followed his glance, saw the dark shapes that wheeled in endless circles against the sun. 'Guess they'll have your bones picked clean in a little while.'

'You're not goin' to kill me,' Dane said and there was something in his voice that jerked the other upright in his saddle. Dane saw the narrowing of the eyes, knew that the other was not quite as sure of himself as he had been earlier.

'Like hell I'm not,' he snapped. His hand reached leisurely for the gun at his hip, fingers closing around the butt, almost caressing it, easing it out of the holster. Dane let him get it clear of the holster before his right hand moved, sweeping down towards his belt. Marty knew now that he had let himself walk into a trap. He had thought that this man had been thoroughly searched before being turned over to him. Now he knew that he had been wrong in this belief. He tried to bring the barrel of the gun up in a sweeping motion, finger tightening on the trigger, a little choking gasp coming from his parted lips as the knife flashed in the air, bright and blue-shining before it embedded itself in his throat. The force of the impact knocked him backward in the saddle, his free hand coming up in front of his face as if to fend off the danger which had already struck him. The choking cry became a low, bubbling moan. He reeled forward, striving to hold life in his eyes, to force it into the muscles of his arm, to squeeze off even one shot from the gun in his hand. A sudden deluge of red trickled down his chest. His eyes began to glaze, but somehow, he found the last ounce of strength in his body to pull the trigger. The single shot bucketed in the stillness and the echoes went bouncing from the canyon walls, diminishing slowly. But even as he had pulled the trigger, Marty was reeling back in the saddle, swaying drunkenly, eyes rolling in his head. The bullet cut through the air six inches above Dane's head, went scudding into the distance at his back. Marty slid from the saddle, hit the ground like an empty sack and rolled over the sharp lip of the gulley, his body crashing down through the stunted bushes and mesquite until it reached the bottom. Dane sat still in the saddle, rubbing feeling back into his wrists, although when it came, when the circulation was restored, the pain bit through him and he winced from stiffness, flexing his fingers experimentally. He made a cigarette, smoked it slowly and looked up at the sky. The vultures were still there, dropping a little lower in their wheeling circles, although he knew they would not come down until he had ridden off.

First, however, there was one thing he had to do. He needed the guns that Marty had been wearing. One of them would still be clutched in his fist, the other in the holster. He waited until the cigarette between his lips was small, then dropped it into the dirt, slid from the saddle and ground it out with his heel. Cautiously, he moved to the edge of the gully, looked down where Marty's body had fallen. He could not see it from where he stood, but the trail of shattered branches and small bushes that had been torn bodily from the face of the gully, indicated where it had fallen. Gingerly, he eased himself down the slope, sucking in his breath sharply every time his raw, bleeding wrists caught against the rough ground, the out-thrusting boulders that jutted from the rocky face.

It took him fifteen minutes to reach the bottom and the sweat was dripping from his forehead by the time he made it, running into his eyes, half blinding him. He paused, looking about him. Marty's body had fallen between two of the bushes, was wedged tightly between them. Getting the Colt from its holster was an easy enough job, but the other was a different proposition. Marty's fingers had clamped around it in his dying moments and it took all of Dane's strength to prise them apart. He was breathing heavily by the time he began the upward climb, hauling himself up, hand over hand, forcing every muscle in his body to the point of exhaustion. Getting one elbow hooked over the rim of the gully, he reached up and anchored himself there with both arms. For a long moment, he hung there, feeling a harsh pain in his chest, digging his toes in against the gully wall in a vain attempt to find any foothold that would enable him to lever himself up over the top. Desperately, he kicked hard at the yielding surface of the rock, managed to chip a little of it away with the toes of his boots, until he managed to find lodgement for his toes. Sucking in a great gulp of air, acutely aware of the weakness in his body, he heaved himself upward in a single convulsive movement that carried him at last, over the rim and on to the flat ground at the top, where he lay flat on his face, trying to draw sufficient air into his starved lungs to clear his head.

His body was afire with cuts and scratches and the light of the setting sun, glinting brilliantly in his eyes, sent blinding flashes of pain through his skull. He knew he had to move, had to force himself to get to his feet and back on that horse, still waiting beside the mesquite bushes. The homesteaders, if they had answered Victoria Maller's call would be assembled at the Maller place, but they would need his help if they were to stand off the men that Skinner had to back him up. Rolling over, he grunted with annoyance at the pain in his limbs, and staggered to his feet. His wrists were torn and bloodied, hands numb and his shirt was torn where he had slithered and bumped down the steep slope after Marty. But he was no longer unarmed.

Somehow, he got back atop the bay, stirred the animal out of its drowsiness with a touch of the spurs, and rode back along the trail he had come. There had been a narrow stream, he remembered, less than a couple of miles back and he reined his horse and dismounted as he came in sight of it. The cold water stung the raw flesh of his wrists and he gritted his teeth as he washed the congealed blood from them. Fortunately there was very little fresh bleeding. Drinking his fill, he waited impatiently for the horse to drink, then swung himself up into the saddle again, kept a roving vigil as he approached the Skinner spread, loping across the open flats that bordered the southern flank of the ranchland. He made it safely through the range of serrated hills where lava boulders were piled like huge marbles across the trail. As he approached the ranch, he let his gaze wander from side to side, looking for movement, but seeing none. Skirting around the grasslands close to the ranch, he moved up towards the hills where he had been surprised earlier. Down below, there was a solitary yellow light showing in one of the windows of the ranch overlooking the courtyard, but there was no sign of any of the horses in the corral or tied to the hitching rail and he sucked in his lips sharply as he realized that the Skinner riders had already pulled out, were on their way to the Maller homestead.

How far had the others travelled? he wondered. They might have a start on him of several miles. He knit his brows in puzzled concentration. Skinner had told Marty to get back in a hurry, to be there to ride out with them. Why had he pulled out so quickly, without waiting for the gunman? Puzzled, but not worried, he swung across the trail and through the trees that clustered on top of the ridge. Moving out of them a little while later, he saw plenty of sign that men had ridden that way recently.

There was a deep and strangely nerve-tingling silence in the hills as he headed across country, hoping to make up time on the riders ahead of him. Behind him, as he wheeled in a wide curve over the flats, the flaming disc of the sun sank down behind a wide horizon that was as red as the sun itself. But the colours faded swiftly once it had gone down. The world became a blue, cool place with long, deep shadows on every side. Dimly, he was aware of faint sounds, just at the limit of his hearing. The hills and ridges now seemed to be filled with the murmuring echoes of men riding the winding trails. They were sounds he couldn't define and the prickling sense of uneasiness in his mind increased as he put spurs to his mount, forcing it on at a punishing pace. He wasn't sure how he could help the homesteaders when he did arrive on the scene. Certainly Skinner's force outnumbered theirs by almost three-to-one; long odds when one considered that the cattle crews were all trained gunmen, professional killers, most of them wanted men who were hidden and sheltered from the law by men such as Ed Skinner, so long as they served his purpose and did all of his dirty work for him.

It was all so appallingly simple. The homesteaders would be wiped out in this range war, the sheriff of El Amaro, working hand in glove with the cattlemen, would take no action and by the time a lethargic Government in Washington got around to doing something about it, it would be far too late, the cattlemen would have moved in, strengthened their stranglehold on the country and nobody would be in a position to oust them from the territory.

He rode steadily through the hills until he was south of the valley, stayed on the top of a small blister of ground only long enough to make sure that he was not being tracked, then put his mount down the shallow slope. The night air had revived him, enabled him to think more clearly and the pain in his wrists had subsided into a dull ache. Now, he could flex his fingers and he checked the guns in his holsters once more, eyes probing the dimness of the valley floor. The Maller homestead lay less than three miles from this edge of the valley. The trail went along a side-hill and angled downward to a little arroyo, then worked its way around the side of a huge, out-thrust boulder which almost blocked the trail. In the darkness, it was difficult to pick out any sign along the trail, but here and there, he came across a patch of earth that had been scuffed by the hoofs of many horses.

As the trail eased northward away from him towards the hills on the other side of the valley, he leaned forward in the saddle, and the bay took its cue and went into a quick lope. Then he was atop a small knoll, the earth churned dusty and rancid by the hoofs of horses. He thinned his lips in satisfaction, nodded to himself and prepared to move down into the valley proper, threw a quick glance over his shoulder, then froze in the saddle. The two hardriding men came spurring from a bunch of trees less than half a mile behind him. He reined in and watched them closely for a few moments. They did not seem to have seen him, but they were using the same trail as he was. From that distance, it was impossible to tell whether they were two more of Skinner's men riding hard to be in at the kill, or a couple of homesteaders riding to Maller's aid. Either way, it was essential that he should make sure before they caught up with him.

The little arroyo was a strategic place here and he made for it, slid from the horse, dismounting on the fly. Crouching down in the thick, tangled bushes, he was ready and waiting when the men came pounding along the trail, slowing their mounts as they neared the sharply-angled bend directly ahead. Then he stepped out of his hiding place, the Colts levelled on them, both cocked and as rock steady as the gaze that locked with theirs.

'Hold up, men,' he said sharply.

The two men hauled up on their reins sharply, one horse rearing high into the air, pawing upward with its forelegs, startled by his sudden appearance. The man on the second mount sat quite still in the saddle for a moment, then his right hand began to move downward.

'Don't try it!' Dane snapped. 'You look like some of Ed Skinner's bunch to me, ridin' out to shoot up the Maller place.'

The man froze instinctively, recognizing the menace in Dane's tone. He let his hand fall loosely on to the saddle-horn in front of him, sucking air into his lungs, in a sharp, explosive gasp.

'That's better. Now dump the guns. Slow and easy.'

The two men hesitated and the man whose mount had reared at his appearance, said tautly: 'You ain't one o' them homesteaders, mister. Just what is this to you?'

'Just shuck the guns or you'll find out the hard way.' Dane told him. He kept the Colts trained on them as they eased their own weapons from their holsters and let them drop with dull thuds on to the ground.

Dane studied them closer. Hard-featured men. He knew the breed inside-out; treacherous and totally undependable, men whose only law was the sixgun and who sold their guns to the highest bidder. They would turn on Skinner as quickly as on anyone else, provided that someone offered them a better price than he did. Not really gunmen — just killers, coldblooded and hard drinkers.

'If you've got an interest in this, mister, reckon you'd better speak out and say so. Skinner will have your hide if he discovers about this.'

Dane gave a dry little chuckle. 'Skinner's already tried to get rid of me. Not once, but several times. He ain't succeeded yet.' He saw the frown come to the taller man's face as the other tried to place him, then noticed the growing look of awareness, the narrowing of the eyes.

'It's that *hombre*, Averill!' he snarled to his companion. There was a note of sheer amazement in his voice. 'But Marty was to — '

'Marty made the same kind of mistake that other men have made when they tried to kill me,' said Dane dispassionately. 'He figured it was goin' to be easy. He paid for his mistake, just as you two will.'

'You killed Marty.' There was an incredulous disbelief in the shorter man's tone. 'I don't believe it.'

'You figure he just let me go?'

There was a little pause. Then the short man suddenly put spurs to his horse's flanks, sent it lunging forward at Dane. Taken by surprise at the sudden, unexpected move, Dane leapt to one side of the narrow trail. The horse lashed at him with its feet. One hoof slammed against the rock within a couple of inches of his body, brought a slide of powdered rock down on to the trail. Then the man had driven his mount past him, was thundering off along the trail, with his companion gigging his own horse along the trail.

Swiftly, Dane snapped a shot at the leading man, saw him lurch in the saddle, hands clinging tightly to the reins in an effort to remain upright, knew that the slug had found its mark, but whether it had been a killing shot, he did not know. The second man leaned from the saddle as he tried to move by, swung a bunched fist that took Dane at the side of the head before he could swing back out of reach. The horse pushed against him, crushing him against the hard rock at his back. One gun was torn from his hand by the weight of the animal, but he managed to retain a grip on the other, bringing it up in a swift, instinctive movement, finger tightening on the trigger convulsively at the same moment.

The deafening din of the gunshot roared at his ears and the powder flash bloomed orange in the darkness of the trail. Whinnying shrilly, the horse stumbled and went down. Dust was a silver screen through which he saw the rider slide agilely from the saddle. The unhorsed rider rolled to one side, came to his feet a moment later, struggled around and struck out with his fist again, catching Dane in the throat, sending him staggering back against the rocks. Fighting for breath, dropping the gun, Dane swung a punch straight up from his belt, caught the man flush on the chin, driving him away in a spinning turn. Desperately, he sucked air into his lungs. His wrists and arms were on fire and there was a dull pain in his throat, spreading down into his chest.

The gunman moved in, squaring up. Too late, Dane saw that he did not intend to use his fists, that this move had been merely a feint for what he really meant to do. The other's foot lashed out, caught Dane on the shin. He went down, stumbling backward, his heels catching in the loose rocks strewn on the trail. Even as he hit the ground he was rolling instinctively away and the second kick never landed. Instead, as the other struck out, Dane caught a tightfisted grip on his heel, held on and twisted savagely, taking the other off his feet.

With a supreme effort, he rose to his feet. The gunman was thrusting himself upright as Dane waited for him, striving to focus his vision on him. The man came charging in, swinging wildly. Stepping to one side, Dane swung, putting all of his weight and strength behind the blow. The man's eyes glittered with the killing fever as he came crowding in. Then Dane's blow caught him on the side of the head. He swayed for a moment, striving to remain on his feet. Then as he flopped forward, Dane clasped both of his hands together and hammered them down on to the back of the man's neck. A lesser neck would have cracked immediately under the force of that blow. As it was, the other uttered a shrill bleat of pain, then collapsed at Dane's feet, knocked out completely. Pulling himself upright, Dane brushed the hair from his eyes, narrowed his eyes, stared down at the inert figure which lay at his feet. Plucking the guns from the man's holsters, he sent them spinning over the side of the trail into the mesquite and sage. The other would give no trouble for some time, he decided; and at the moment, there was no time to waste. The other man may have ridden on ahead and warned Skinner of what had happened and he would ride into trouble when he moved on.

Shaking his head in an attempt to clear it, he found and holstered the guns he had dropped, caught his horse and pulled himself up into the saddle. The wind flowing down the side of the trail was a cool pressure, reviving him as he rode into the darkness. A quarter of a mile along the trail he knew that Skinner had not been warned of his presence there. The short gunman lay face-downward at a bend in the trail, his arms outflung and his legs twisted under him. He had evidently collapsed and fallen from his mount, which had gone running on along the trail. Dane paused only long enough to ascertain that the other was dead, then rode on.

A little later, he crossed the wide road that led through the valley and the dust stayed with him as he rode, to indicate other travel close at hand; and the silence of the hills on either side of the valley had in it the tag-ends of sounds which had not quite faded out completely and he got the distinct impression of men still riding along narrow trails, all of them in front of him, men riding with their urgent hastes and purposes.

A quarter of an hour brought him on top of the pasture land that rose above the homestead. Everything was strangely familiar now and he knew exactly where he was. It was here that he caught the distant break of gunfire from down in the meadow fronting the Maller place. The firing stayed brisk as he tried to pick out the full intensity and direction of it. The wind carried it towards him and he guessed that it was further away than he would normally have placed it. He rode with a cautious slowness down the slope, making no sound. Now that he was in sight of the homestead, he could pick out the flashes of the guns, faint pinpricks of light in the darkness. He looked anxiously at the shadowed trail that wound down past the small herd on the brow of the hill, bedded down for the night. As yet, nobody in Skinner's band had thought of stampeding them, but the idea would come soon and there was no doubt they would act on it.

The cattle made no sound as he rode past them. Unpredictable brutes at the best of times, they might have set up a strident bellowing which would have warned the men down below. The moon came out from behind a bank of low cloud, flooded the valley with soft yellow light. This was as far as he could safely go on horseback. Dismounting, he checked the guns once more, then moved forward in the dimness. He had a momentary creepy feeling as the blasting roar of gunfire burgeoned up once more and by the muzzle flashes, he could see that the main concentration of fire was on this side of the homestead. Skinner had positioned his men so that they were between the herd, the main trail over the hill, and the house itself, thereby cutting off any further help which might be riding to Maller's aid. Other men had fanned out and had surrounded the buildings, the barns and stockade, but they were strung out thinly on the ground, were there merely to make certain that none of the men inside the buildings succeeded in slipping away in the moonlit darkness.

Dane tightened his lips, screwed up his eyes to take in the whole picture. It was simple to visualize Skinner's plan. He meant to wear down the defenders and then use his overwhelming force to rush the place. He had all night in which to do it, and plenty of men. It might be a different proposition if they were forced to wait until daylight before they could attack — then the advantage would lie with the defenders, but it was unlikely that the uneven battle would last that long.

Every muscle in him was strung so tight that his body began to ache again and there was the knotting agony of cramp in his legs as he lay flat on the wet grass, holding himself absolutely still. His eyes studied the dark folds of the ground in front of him. Gently, he worked his way forward, every sense alert for trouble. Then he paused. He wasn't sure what had brought to him that faint chill of warning — maybe the mere remembering that Skinner might not be such a fool as to leave the trail behind him unguarded.

He froze suddenly. Instinct made him deny his body's demand for more movement to ease the tight claws of cramp. The faint spark of brightness on the very edge of his vision came again. The light may have been a reflection in one of the windows of the homestead, but then it came once more and he knew what it was; not the brief scratch of light from a match, but the more steady, more contained light which came from the redly glowing tip of a cigarette as a man drew deeply on it, with a hand cupped over it in an attempt to hide the intermittent glow.

He felt a grim amusement. A sentry should be more careful than that, he thought, although the other probably considered himself to be quite safe. But a man could die, quite easily, making a mistake such as that. With a painful slowness he slithered forward, keeping his head low; an old trick which enabled him to pick out a man against the skyline. He saw the man a few moments later, seated on a low outcrop of ground, facing him, occasionally pausing to lift his head and peer into the dimness. It was almost as if he were looking straight at him, yet the sentry gave no sign of seeing him. An inch at a time, he edged off the trail, working his way around the other. He did not begrudge the extra seconds it took, knowing that in moonlit darkness, with plenty of shadows around, the eye could easily pick out a sudden, jerky movement, whereas a slow, creeping shadow would not be seen. While he was slithering forward, his mind worked over a series of moves, assessing them and rejecting those which were too dangerous in the circumstances. When he finally swung back to the trail, he came up behind the other, his feet gathered under him, the Colt in his hand reversed, so that he gripped it tightly by the barrel. He could not afford to take the risk of shooting the other down. A gunshot from this direction would carry easily in the darkness in spite of the racket from around the buildings less than three hundred yards away.

Some hidden instinct seemed to warn the man of his danger as Dane rose silently from the grass at his back. He half swung, tried to lift an arm to defend himself, his lips opening to give a warning yell. But the shout was never uttered. The butt of the pistol crashed down on the side of his head and he collapsed forward with a low moan, crumpling to the ground at Dane's feet.

Now there was no time to be lost. Dane did not think that Skinner would have left any other men behind to guard the trail, relying on this one man to give any warning of trouble.

A group of men crashed away through the brush less than twenty yards in front of him at a sudden, barked order. Dane crouched down, quivering a little. Those men had been so close to him and he hadn't been aware of their presence in the shadows. He began to inch forward, flattened himself under a clump of dusty mesquite, mindless of the rough, bare branches that raked his face and hands. For a moment, he lay motionless, every nerve in his body tingling at the narrow margin by which he had escaped detection. A savage volley of gunfire from his right broke out suddenly as the group which had just moved in opened fire on the occupants of the house.

Carefully, he eased the guns from their holsters, moved forward a couple of yards until he reached a point where his eyes were able to make out small, inconsequential movements among the shadows. He located the nearer edge of the corral, the line of wooden posts stretching round in a wide, sweeping curve. A handful of ponies at the far side kicked their heels at the racket.

Off to the right were the two barns and beyond them the house itself, long and low-roofed. Sparks of orange flame came from the windows and he saw that there were at least a couple of men crouched down on the porch, firing into the shadows beyond the corral where a bunch of the cattle crew were.

Using what concealment he could, he came up behind the men firing at the barns. So far, they were not aware of his presence. Slowly, he came to his knees, feeling the urge to forget caution as he lined up the guns on the men among the shadows. It was not his nature to shoot men in the back and his first shot went over their crouching heads. He had them all placed clearly now and as they whirled, turned to meet the new menace at their backs, he sent shot after shot into them, saw half a dozen of them keel over as the slugs bit deep into their bodies.

The shooting on the far side of the homestead went on at random. Nobody there seemed to be taking the least notice of what was happening here. A couple of bullets slammed through the branches of the mesquite with a faintly heard rustling and he pulled his head down, crawled to one side, lay on his shoulder as he thrust more cartridges into the empty chambers of the guns. He heard the harsh yelling grow in magnitude as the men realized that they had been bushwhacked from the rear. Someone was shouting orders at the top of his voice, but against the racket of gunfire from further away it was impossible to tell if it was Skinner, or his foreman.

More firing rose in a smothering racket from the direction of the barns where a bunch of the homesteaders were holed up. They had realized that something was happening here, something which they did not quite understand, but the volume of fire along this particular stretch of the corral had slackened abruptly and even if they did not know the exact reason for it, they knew that this was their chance to take the offensive, before Skinner could rally his men from the other side of the homestead.

Breathing heavily, Dane slithered a couple of yards along the narrow gully, lifted his head a cautious inch, eyes narrowed. The main weight of fire still seemed to press against the barns and the front of the house so that for the moment slugs were beating against the walls and doors of the buildings. Rising carefully to his hands and knees, Dane crawled on. A handful of men ran fast and clumsy around the perimeter of the corral. In the pale moonlight, he could just make them out as they darted towards the porch. They were halfway over the stretch of open ground when the volley of fire from the porch beat them back, leaving five of the men stretched out in the centre of the dusty courtyard, unmoving humps of shadow. The others ran back for the cover of the corral, went down out of sight.

It was beginning to look as if the cattlemen were not having this fight all their own way, he thought grimly. Maybe, after all, Skinner had bitten off more than he could chew when he had ridden against this place. Perhaps he had figured that few, if any, of the other nesters would rally round and fight. It was difficult to estimate how many men the girl had managed to bring into this fight but from the volume of fire, he reckoned there were at least thirty, possibly more, in the house and barns, and they were giving a good account of themselves. Maybe all was not lost, he reflected tautly.

He crawled over the rough ground, drew himself forward so that he was less than ten feet from the corral fence, and waited tightly. Nothing happened. No one seemed to be here now, but bullets were scudding into the dirt close by, bullets from the defenders in the barn and he moved cautiously back, not wanting to be shot by one of the homesteaders.

Circling behind Skinner's men, he cast about him, looking for the place where they had tethered their mounts. If he could stampede them away, there was a chance they could finish them all, right here and now. At first, he could see no sign of the horses, although he guessed that Skinner would have ridden down close to the homestead before he gave the order to dismount, confident of his own superiority in numbers.

Then he caught a glimpse of them, high up on a small knoll of ground to his left. The shouting and yelling and shooting went on around the buildings at his back as he made his way up the slope. Ten yards from the line of horses, he caught a glimpse of the guard. Drawing back into the shadow, he paused for a moment, saw that the man's attention had been caught by the firing going on down in the depths of the valley. Drawing himself up to his full height, keeping a tight grip on the barrel of the gun in his hand, he walked brazenly towards the line of horses. The man swung round, peered into the darkness. Still not suspicious, he said harshly: 'Ed want the horses taken down now?'

'Sure,' muttered Dane hoarsely.

'Figured he might. Sounds as if they've got too many for us to handle down there. He'll be best advised to pull out and try again when we've rounded up all of the boys.'

'Guess so,' Dane lowered his head, the brim of his hat pulled well down, as he moved towards the horse nearest the guard. 'He was told that before we pulled out, but he wouldn't listen. Maybe now, he'll know how many men he needs to finish off these nesters.'

He worked his way slowly around the side of the horse, the gun poised in his hand, not once taking his eyes off the man in front of him. The other bent forward to slacken off the rope that hitched the horses together. He had no chance to turn his head or cry out before the butt of the gun struck him behind the ear. Dane caught his body as he slumped forward, lowered it slowly to the ground, then untied the rope, slapped the horses on the rumps, sending them racing away down the knoll, away from the scene of firing.

When he got down the slope again, approaching the homestead, it was to find that it was nearly over. The cattlemen were finished. Skinner had considered himself to be unbeatable, had never thought that the homesteaders would form a solid front against him, would fight him on ground of their own choosing. A little sporadic firing still came from the north of the house, but everywhere else, the cattlemen and their crews were finished.

Most of the trail drovers had either been killed or wounded. Somehow, in the confusion, Ed Skinner and a handful of his men had got away. Without horses, they would make slow progress getting out of the valley on foot.

Dane made his way to the house, looking about him intently in the darkness. As he approached the porch, the girl came out, caught sight of him and walked over to him. Her face was tight, still with that curiously indrawn look, but she gave him a weary smile as she came up to him.

'We fought them off,' she said quietly. 'Was that you back there who took a bunch of them from behind?'

He nodded. Briefly, he told her what had happened, how he had been caught on the ridge overlooking the Skinner ranch and how Marty had been ordered to take him out and kill him. She listened in silence, the expression on her face unchanging. When he had finished, she looked off into the moonlit distance, lips placed tightly together, brows drawn down a little over her eyes. 'Ed Skinner must have got away in the distance. We can't find any sign of him.'

'He won't get too far on foot,' Dane murmured. 'I scared off all of their horses. They'll be scattered to the end of the valley and beyond by now. He'll never catch any of them.'

'And his men?' she queried.

'I reckon he's finished. You've broken

him. The cattlemen are all busted up. I don't reckon you have anythin' to fear from Ed Skinner now, even if he makes it back to his own spread. He'll never get any more men to ride with him against you.'

'Perhaps you're right.' Her voice was suddenly weary. 'I hope so, for all our sakes. We want to live in peace, not to be constantly at war with our neighbours.'

'This ought to please you then,' said Dane, his eyes fixed on her face, watching the play of emotions there.

'It does,' she said. Her voice was oddly cold and distant. 'But I wish I could be as sure of the future as you are.'

He gave a slight shrug of his shoulders. 'The future for me is still dark. I've still got some business to settle in El Amaro. Somethin' that has nothin' to do with Skinner.'

'You're still determined to hunt down this man and kill him?' It was more of a statement than a question, as if she had already read on his face what was in his mind. Her face was as blank as his now, watching, waiting, with an awareness of his presence there, but little else.

'Do you think it would be any use warnin' the sheriff of what I know?'

She shook her head. 'If you do that, you're a fool. I know these people in town. He'll have you put in jail and then, one night, you'll be shot, trying to escape.'

5

Jailbreak

Sheriff Keeler ran his gaze over Dane, his face tight. He said thickly: 'You seem to be mighty anxious to get yourself killed.' His brows drew together. 'Say, you weren't in that ruckus at the Maller place a couple of nights ago, were you?'

'Could be,' Dane was non-committal. 'You goin' to take action against those homesteaders? If you're considerin' it, I'd advise you to forget it.'

'Now see here, I don't take kindly to threats like that,' Keeler stepped forward a pace. 'I don't know why I'm tryin' to help you like this. I told you before that I didn't want any trouble in town.'

'You think I had anythin' to do with that trouble between the nesters and the ranchers?'

'I'm not sure. If I thought that, I wouldn't hesitate to put you in jail. But I want you out of this territory before anythin' else happens.'

Dane shook his head slowly, meaningly. 'I aim to get my business finished before I ride out.'

Keeler swung to stare out of the window. 'This business of yours. Anythin' to do with killin' a man?'

'That's my concern.'

Keeler's surprise came under quick control and his eyes narrowed with a surge of suspicion. He swung away from the window. 'You try to shoot down anyone in El Amaro and you'll stir up more than you can handle. I'll give you more than Skinner did those nesters; I'll give you fair warnin' to stay out of anythin' like that. Any feud between you and some other *hombre* can wait until you're out of town. I won't have gunfighting in my town.'

'This is out of your hands, Sheriff,' Dane said tightly. He stepped to the door. 'I came here to find a man who did me a wrong. That's my right and I don't know of any law against it. I'm not leavin' without finishing this.'

His eyes held the sheriff's steadily. There was something here that he didn't quite understand. Keeler's nervousness and his sudden anger. Did the other suspect the real reason he was here in El Amaro? If he did, he showed little of it. Turning, Dane opened the door and stepped out on to the boardwalk.

Walking across the street, be stepped into the saloon. It was cool here in contrast to the dusty heat of the street. The bar stretched from one side of the front room to the other. At one end, it ran to the side of a small door that led through into the card room at the rear of the building. There were two mirrors at the back of the bar, blackened a little around the edges; and a lot of small circular tables. It was almost noon and at the moment the saloon was nearly empty. A drunk lay with his head pillowed in his arms across one of the tables, a couple of empty bottles beside his outstretched hand. In one corner, a poker game was in progress. The four men gave him a quick glance, then looked back at their cards, ignoring him.

The bartender came forward, stood with his hands flat on top of the bar as Dane walked up to him. His dark, deep-set eyes watched the other's progress with a barely concealed interest. He prided himself on being a good judge of men, ever since the old days before the war when he had been a gunslick riding with one of the border gangs, terrorizing this territory. A couple of bullets in one of his legs had left him a semi-cripple, his limb twisted so that he could no longer ride, could only just walk. But he had been one of the lucky ones. The others had, sooner or later, bucked with the law and were buried on Boot Hill.

Strangely, the other did not feel bitter about the wound which had left him like this. He had long since ceased to think about the old days. Now he lived for the present, watching the men who came into the saloon, stayed for a little while, and then drifted on again. He had learned a long time ago, to look beneath the mask that most men who came into the saloon wore. Now he eyed the man who stood in front of him, elbows resting on the bar, with critical eyes, although little of this scrutiny showed on his expressionless features.

'Whiskey,' said Dane shortly.

The other said nothing, eyed him for a moment longer, then went a little way along the bar, brought a bottle and glass along and set them down in front of him.

Dane poured himself a drink, gulped it down, felt it hit the back of his throat and then slide down into an expanding hazy, warmth in his stomach. He let his gaze drift lazily from one side of the saloon to the other, then swung back to the bartender.

'You know an *hombre* called Clem Keeler?' he asked casually.

He saw the barman start a little, then catch himself. The other shook his head slowly. 'Never heard of him,' he said shortly. 'You lookin' for somebody by that name?'

'That's right. And I ain't a liar. You know him well enough. The sheriff's son. Goin' to tell me where he is?'

'Mister,' said the other very slowly, obviously choosing his words carefully. 'I don't know who you are, or why you're here. But there are plenty of drifters around town and none of them is the sheriff's son.'

'No?' Dane looked steadily into the other's face. 'You're lyin'.' Dane let the silence come back and settle between them. Pouring out a second glass, he sipped it slowly, staring fixedly at the other over the rim. He saw the other grow more uncomfortable, saw the look of apprehension grow in his eyes. The bartender gave a sharp hitch to his trousers, stepped a pace away from the

208

bar. Then he swallowed thickly, leaned forward conspiratorially, his glance flicking to the men at the nearby table. They were still concentrating on their game and lowering his voice, he muttered: 'All right, stranger. So Clem runs wild with that bunch in the hills. Only his Pa don't know that, you see. Keeler's a good sheriff for El Amaro. And so long as those *hombres* in the hills don't bother us, we ain't goin' to talk against 'em.' Dane tightened his lips. So it was like that, he reflected. He ought to have known that the folk in a cattle town such as this would stick by each other. The outlaws robbed the stage and the freighters who plied between El Amaro and Virginia City. This didn't really affect the trade for the town; and those ranchers who lost a few head of cattle, rustled over the border, they'd shoot if they caught any of the rustlers on their land, but that would be as far as it went.

'Know where I can find him?' Dane asked again.

It was obvious that the other's mind was working; obvious in the flutterings of his hands and fingers as he twisted the damp cloth at his waistband, obvious in the workings of the muscles of his flabby features. 'Yeah, I reckon you might find him over at the hotel. Got a room up there on the top floor. Sometimes has a few friends with him for a game of poker.'

'Ever come into the saloon?'

'Sometimes. Not often.'

'Thanks.' Dane poured another drink, turned away and went outside. The hotel stood a little way along the street and he eyed it carefully before moving on and going inside. The clerk stood behind the desk, the same man he had met earlier. He went over to him. 'You still holdin' my room here?' he asked tightly.

The other glanced up, startled, then nodded his head quickly. 'Why sure, Mister Averill. It's still ready for you.' He reached back and pulled down the key, handing it over the desk.

Dane took it, asked quietly: 'Clem Keeler up in his room?'

'Why yes, but — ' The other stopped short, eyed him sharply. 'I'm not sure,' he stammered. 'I didn't actually see him come in, but if he's in the hotel, I reckon that's where he'll be at this time of day.'

'Good. I'll go up and see him as soon as I've cleaned up. Which room is his?'

For a moment he thought that the other did not intend to answer. Then the clerk said quietly, hesitantly. 'Room right at the back of the top floor. You can't miss it, stands by itself at the end of the corridor.'

'Thanks, I'll manage to find it.' Dane hitched his gunbelt a little higher around his middle, then made his way up the creaking, winding stairs. At the top, he paused, glanced behind him. The clerk was still standing at the back of the desk, staring up after him. As soon as he saw Dane's gaze on him, he looked away sheepishly and pretended to be working with the ledger in front of him. So the clerk was curious too, was he, thought Dane. Well, he didn't expect too much trouble from the other. Evidently, he recognized Dane as some kind of gunfighter, but he wasn't sure why he wanted to see Clem Keeler.

Going into his own room, Dane locked the door, peeled off his dusty shirt and laid out a fresh one from his roll. Then he washed his face and body from the pitcher on the chest of drawers. The cool water cracked the mask of dust and made his flesh sting, but he felt fresher than he had for several days. Pulling on the clean shirt, he left it open at the neck, then buckled the heavy gunbelt around his middle, eased the Colts in their holsters, then stepped out into the corridor. Climbing the other flight of stairs, he soft-footed along the passage at the top. The door of the room at the far end was half open and he heard the soft murmur of voices as he drew nearer. There was a little tingle of excitement in his mind, but he forced it away with an effort. He reached the door, paused just out of sight, his body pressed tightly against the wall. He listened for several seconds, lips tightening as he picked out a voice that was oddly familiar. Slipping one of the Colts from its holster, he hefted it into his right hand, pushed open the door with his left, and stepped through into the room, levelling the gun on the men at the table.

'Sorry to break up this little game, gents,' he said, his voice ominously soft.

The four men turned their heads to stare at him. One man tried to go for his gun, then froze as Dane swung the muzzle of the Colt in his direction. 'That's better.' He let his gaze travel from one man to the other, until it finally rested on Clem Keeler. The outlaw leader's gaze slid away and his face settled into a very faint but unmistakable expression of apprehension. He stared down at the black muzzle of the gun lined up on him.

'These more of your outlaw friends,

Keeler?' Dane asked. The hard eyes flickered ironically over Keeler's face and then went back to the cards on the table, almost as if they were more important. 'You know who I am, Keeler. The man you framed. I swore I'd get you if it was the last thing I did.'

There was a gun on the table in front of Keeler and his gaze flicked towards it.

'If you want to die right now,' Dane said, 'you can make a try for your gun.'

Keeler began to curse savagely. He looked up in quick outrage at the face of the man standing in the doorway. 'You won't kill me, Averill,' he said thickly. 'Not in El Amaro. You'd never get out of town alive if you shot me down in cold blood. And you'd have to kill these men too, if you wanted to be sure there were no witnesses around. You're no fool.' His voice was suddenly normal, as if he were sure of himself now, knew himself to be on familiar ground, something which he figured gave him the advantage. His gaze slid away from Dane's face and he turned deliberately to the three men sitting round the table with him. 'These are all pretty important men in town, Averill, as you can probably see. And I doubt if — '

'Save your breath, Keeler,' grated Dane tightly. 'I aim to take you out of here, out of town. We can settle the score between us where none of your friends will interfere.'

'Probably,' said Keeler, his tone very cool, 'you can handle a gun far better than I can. Seems to me that you've had a lot more practice than I have. I'd be a fool to ride out of town with you, wouldn't I? I'm not goin' with you and if you feel like riskin' your neck and shootin' your ducks on the ground, then go ahead.' He sat back in his chair, taking care to keep his hands well away from the gun on the table.

'I might do that,' grunted Dane. He had the inescapable feeling that the advantage was slipping away from him fast.

Keeler shook his head, his smoothly handsome face twisted into a bland smile. 'I doubt that, Averill. Your kind of killer never likes to shoot it out without gettin' the other man to draw first. Possibly bolsters your ego, makes it possible for you to justify the shootin'. Well, I don't intend to give you that excuse for killin' me.'

'It's more of a chance than you gave me, framin' me for murder and robbery, settin' the law on me across half a dozen states.'

'You can't prove that.' There was the sharp, bright glitter of tight amusement in the other's eyes. He sat quite at ease at the table, supremely confident.

Dane felt the savage anger rising in him. Taking a step forward, he reached out and sent the gun on the table skimming into the corner of the room. 'Better get on your feet, Keeler,' he said sharply. 'Maybe if these so-called friends of yours knew the kind of man you really are, knew of those other friends of yours up in the hills, they might not be so ready and willin' to afford you their protection.'

'I don't know what you're talkin' about,' snapped the other. He grinned thinly, but there was a sudden look of strain narrowing his features.

'Now see here, stranger,' broke in one of the other men, a puffy-faced individual in a black frock coat, mutton-chop whiskers giving him the only look of dignity he possessed. 'I must protest most strongly about this. If this is a hold-up, then as Mister Keeler says, you're a fool. You'll never get away with it and I shall personally see that — '

'Keep out of this,' snapped Dane tautly. 'This is no concern of yours.' He turned back to Keeler. All of the anger that had been boiling and simmering inside him over the past months came to the front of his mind. Stepping forward quickly, he rammed the muzzle of the Colt into Keeler's chest, saw the look of agony on the other's face as he sucked in a gasp of air.

'I won't give you another warnin',' he said thinly. 'On your feet and move over to the door.'

The other hesitated, then got slowly to his feet. His face was a pasty colour but there was murder in his eyes. Dane crowded him as he moved in the direction of the open door.

'That's just fine,' Dane said. He eyed the other coldly, wishing that he could pull the trigger now when it was sure, knowing that the other's mind was working fast, trying to figure out some way out of this. But that kind of killing wasn't in him. Keeler would get his chance when the time came, but there would be nobody else around to change the odds when that happened.

'Warn those friends of yours that if any of them tries anythin', you'll get it first,' he said harshly.

'Do as he says,' Keeler called over his shoulder. He kept his hands well away from his sides. Quickly, as they reached the door, Dane slipped the gun from Keeler's other holster and tossed it along the corridor.

'Now walk down the stairs, slow and easy,' Dane said. 'And pray for your own sake that nobody tries any shootin'.'

Cursing in a low, savage voice, Keeler walked along the corridor, past the other rooms, the doors of which were all closed, and started down the stairs, Dane close behind him. Keeler was unsure of himself now and there were little beads of sweat starting out on his forehead. At the bottom of the stairs, the lobby of the hotel was still and empty. Out of the corner of his eye, Dane saw that there was no sign of the clerk who had earlier been standing behind the desk. Evidently the other had guessed there might be trouble and had slipped out while he had had the chance, not wanting to be caught up in any gunplay.

'When you get outside into the street, walk straight for your horse, saddle up and ride out in front of me,' Dane ordered brusquely, 'and remember that the first wrong move you make will be your last.'

'You still reckon you're goin' to get away with this, Averill,' grunted the other. 'Even if we do ride out of town, how far do you figure you'll get?'

'Far enough to even the score with you,' snapped Dane. 'And once you're dead, I reckon that band of killers you've been leadin' in the hills will be finished.'

He could see the other's mind working. He would be trying to figure out how he could stop Dane before they were out of town. Once they were away from El Amaro, he knew he would have very little chance of getting out of the gunplay that was to come and he was not the sort of man to take on anything like that unless the odds were definitely in his favour.

Keeler paused in front of the door, hand outstretched to push it open. He licked his lips nervously. 'All right,' snapped Dane. 'Outside — and don't try anythin' funny.'

There was a sudden movement at Dane's back. He half turned, but he was not fast enough. Something hard jabbed into the small of his back and a moment later, a voice grated. 'Elevate your hands and drop that gun, Averill.'

Dane paused, the gun muzzle pressed further into his back. Reluctanly, he let the gun drop on to the floor, lifted his hands over his head. Clem Keeler turned, a vicious grin on his face as his father stepped around from behind Dane, the gun in his hand levelled on him. Beside the sheriff was the runty-featured clerk. It was so obvious what had happened that Dane cursed himself for not having considered the possibility. Instead of just getting out of the hotel when he reckoned that trouble was looming up, the clerk had gone straight for the sheriff.

'That's better,' muttered Clem Keeler thinly. He drew back his bunched fist and Dane staggered forward as the blow caught him in the stomach. Another blow hit his head as he went down and pain roared through his brain. He dropped to his knees. Stars burst inside his head and he felt the air rush out of his lungs as Keeler's boot caught him in the chest. Dimly, he heard the sheriff say: 'Reckon that's enough, Clem. Let him get up now and we'll haul him off to jail.'

'Sure, sure,' grunted the other, lips twisted back into a snarling smile. 'I guess that's the fit place for a killer like this. He was aimin' to get me out of town and shoot me down in cold blood. Ask Jeb and the others upstairs. They heard every word, every threat he made.'

Painfully, Dane dragged himself up on to his hands and knees, shook his head in an attempt to clear it. He had walked straight into a trap and at the moment, there seemed to be no way out of it. Slowly, the roaring in his head went away and he was able to focus his vision on things around him. The lobby ceased spinning and he felt hands grab him by the arms and pull him roughly to his feet. He stood swaying for several moments, an agonizing throbbing at the back of his eyes. With an effort, he fought back to clarity. He had trouble in standing straight and when he moved, his legs and ankles rocked as if unable to bear his weight, too weak to support him properly.

'All right, Averill. I reckon we'll take a walk over to the jail,' grunted the sheriff. 'Better come quietly. We don't take to attempted murder in this town; not when it concerns my son.'

Dane sucked air through his open mouth, forced his blurring vision to clear. He made out Clem's face as it swam into focus. There was a look of triumph on it and he knew that he had failed. Once they got him inside that jail, it would mean the end for him; there was nothing as sure as that. Somehow, a lynch mob would be formed, if the outlaws themselves didn't ride into town to bust him out and string him up from the nearest tree.

Stumbling, he was forced through the

door and out into the street. A small group of people had gathered on the boardwalk. They watched, interested, as he was taken to the jail.

Inside the cell at the rear of the building, he sat down heavily on the low, iron bed. The door clanged shut with a sound of finality and he dimly heard the footsteps of the sheriff fading into the distance along the narrow passage, and then the sound of the door at the far end closing. He had no sense of time and he didn't know whether he sat on the edge of the bed for one minute or ten. The brutal beating he had taken had left his feelings numb as well as his body. Sitting there, staring straight in front of him, he saw himself in far sharper perspective than before. He ought to have shot down Clem Keeler while he had had the chance. At least if he had done that, there would have been the deep sense of satisfaction in knowing that even if he paid with his own life, he had fulfilled his errand of vengeance. Now, no one in town would believe him if he tried to tell them that the sheriff's son was a vicious killer, the man who led the wolf pack in the hills, the man who walked openly in the streets of El Amaro, getting all of the information which enabled them to know when to strike at stage or freight wagon.

When Keeler brought him some food, there was a deputy with him who stood at the door of the cell, keeping a Winchester trained on him. Evidently they were taking no chances with him; and Dane wondered what sort of story Clem had told his father about him.

Keeler placed the tin next to the bed, then stepped back. Going outside, he locked the door and stood for a moment, staring in, a curious expression on his face.

'You know, Averill,' he said at last, 'I knew there was somethin' about your face that I recognized. Wasn't until Clem went through some of the old posters and notices with me an hour ago, that we came across your picture.

Seems you're a wanted man, Averill. Guess I ought to have known it when you first rode into town.' He paused, then went on: 'Ain't you got nothin' to say in your defence, Averill?'

'What I've got to say, Sheriff, you'd never believe.'

The other stared at him for several moments, then turned and walked off, the deputy following him.

* ★ *

It was still dark when Dane woke. The bed on which he lay was hard and uncomfortable and he rolled over on to his side, trying to ignore the flooding ache in his stomach. The muscles were still tender and sore where Clem Keeler had punched him. After a while, he sat up. This eased the pain a little and he dug in his pocket for the making of a smoke. Everything was quiet outside. Through the tiny window in the wall he could make out a rectangular patch of sky, with a handful of bright stars shining against it. The town was quiet and asleep; but what was Clem Keeler doing at that moment? he wondered. Was he asleep too, or was he up there in the hills, getting his men together, ready to ride down and make sure, once and for all, that Dane Averill did no more talking, was no longer dangerous?

The smoke brought a little of the warmth back into his chest, eased the throbbing pain in his head. There was the crusty feeling of dried blood on the side of his face and he touched it gingerly with his fingers, wincing a little as pain lanced through his cheek. The silence only served to accentuate the feeling of danger in his mind, sharpened his senses. Somewhere, he heard the faint snicker of a horse. He went over to the small window set in the wall some two feet above his head. Glancing back he tugged experimentally at the iron bed, found to his surprise that it was not bolted to the floor as he had expected, or if it had been, the metal of the bolts had sheared away with the long passage of time. Ignoring the pain in his arms and legs, he pulled the bed over to the wall beneath the window and climbed up, balancing himself so that he could just see through the barred window. The narrow alley outside looked deserted, with long, moon-thrown shadows lying across it Then, at the far end, where it joined the main street, he saw the flicker of movement, knew he had not been mistaken when it came again, closer this time.

There was a sudden tightness in his throat as he watched that shadow moving nearer. Had Keeler decided that he had lived long enough? Was this one of his men moving in silently for the kill, a quick shot through this window into the body of a sleeping man? Quickly, he looked about him for a weapon — anything he could use to defend himself. There was nothing. In the dimness, he made out the dark figure that came along the alley, paused across from the rear of the jail, then darted across the open patch of ground, through the yellow moonlight and for the first time, Dane caught a clear glimpse of the other.

'Victoria!' He called the girl's name softly, felt a thrill of surprise run through him. She was the last person he had expected to see here.

The girl came up to the outside wall, peered up at the window. 'No noise,' she said tightly. 'We'll have you out of there presently.'

'How do you figure on doin' it?' he asked, fingers curled around the metal bars. They felt solid, set in the material of the wall itself.

'You'll see.' She stepped closer to the wall so that he could not see her, but her voice drifted up to him from just below the window. 'Reach out if you can and take this.'

He thrust his hand between the vertical bars, straining his fingers down as far as he could. They touched hard, cold metal, curled about it, drew the gun back into the jail. Now that he was no longer unarmed, he felt a growing sense of elation in him. He still did not doubt that there was a night marshal on duty in the outer office, with possibly a couple of deputies, to see that he did not escape. Going over to the door of the cell, he pressed himself against it, listened intently for any sound that might reach him from the outer office. For a long moment, almost two minutes, he could hear nothing. No sound reached him from the end of the passage. Then he heard the faint scrape of a chair as it was pushed back on the floor, the dull murmur of voices speaking in a low undertone. After that, there was silence for a long moment, a silence broken by the creak as the door at the far end of the passage was opened. Footsteps sounded, echoing hollowly in the darkness. Two men stood in front of him, peering through the door, then one began to fit the keys in his hand into the heavy lock, trying one after the other, until he got the right one and the door swung open.

'Reckon we'd better get out of here and fast,' grunted one of the men. He closed the cell door, locked it, then tossed the bunch of keys inside. In the outer office, there was an oil lamp still burning on the table. Two men lay unconscious on the floor in front of the desk. Dane gave them both a quick glance. One was a deputy he had seen around town earlier. The other was a stranger to him. That meant the sheriff was asleep somewhere in town, unaware of what had happened. Dane smiled grimly to himself as he went out into the street, stood for a moment, drawing the cold night air down into his lungs. The girl came around the corner of the building a moment later, leading a couple of horses.

'How did you know I was in jail?' he said, taking the reins from her and swinging himself up into the saddle.

'Time enough to talk about that when we're well out of El Amaro,' said the girl quickly. 'There may be more trouble and we have to ride fast if we're to be out of danger.'

He nodded swiftly. There was a lot of truth in her words. Sooner or later, that empty cell and those two unconscious men were going to be found and not only the sheriff and his posse, but those outlaws from the hills, led by Clem Keeler would be on his trail. They rode out of town, walking their mounts until they had cleared the outskirts, then up the slope at a slow run. After they had passed a bend in the trail, running around it, they found themselves facing another sharp rise, their horses slowing as they made the upgrade. The trees about them softened any sounds from a lower level. In the moonlight, the trail was a pale grey scar that wound in and out of rocky inclines, across level stretches of ground, through clumps of sage and cactus and into heavy timber.

Dane's mind was functioning clearly now. The situation was changed drastically from what it had been a few days before. Now, he was no longer completely alone in this country, or in this fight. The nesters seemed to feel that they owed him something for aiding them against Ed Skinner and his crew. They were all shrewd, hard, relentless men, who stuck together and never forgot a favour. The kind of friends a man sought and very rarely found.

He edged his mount forward until he was riding beside the girl. They were now well clear of El Amaro, out in open range country, safe for the time being from posse or outlaws.

'You still haven't told me how you knew where I was,' he said quietly.

The girl turned her head. The bright yellow moonlight touched the long hair on her shoulders, where it came from beneath the wide-brimmed hat, filling it with rich golden highlights. 'We have a few friends in town,' she explained. 'When you were taken from the hotel and across to the jail, one of them saw what happened and rode in to warn us. It didn't take long to figure out what had really taken place, especially when we heard that Clem

Keeler had been there. You tried to even the score with him, didn't you?'

'Yes.' The word was tight in his mouth. 'I had him cold. I should have shot him down then, when he was in front of my gun. But I figured I'd give him an even break, which is more than he ever did for any man. I meant to ride him out of town and give him a chance to draw . . .'

'What went wrong?'

'The lobby clerk informed the sheriff and he turned up on the scene in the hotel. Naturally, he ain't goin' to take my word against his son's. Not when there was a picture of me on a wanted notice in his office.'

'So that was it.' She nodded her head slowly. 'I thought it would have to be something like that. And now you'll have the law and the lawless hunting you down, waiting for a chance to kill you.'

'I know. The only chance I've got now is to ride out after Keeler — and this time, I won't make the same mistake again.'

'You're riding after him alone?' There was surprise and concern in her voice.

'Sometimes, a lone rider makes better time than a bunch of men,' Dane said. He stared ahead of him, watched the moon drift slowly into a thin haze of cloud, then sail out again into the clear night sky.

'You know best,' murmured the girl. 'Would it make any difference if I were to tell you that I don't want you to go, that there's a job for you any time with us and that with Skinner finished, you'll be safe there.'

'At the moment, it won't make any difference,' Dane said tautly. 'While Keeler is alive, I won't be safe. One of us has got to die — and soon.'

The girl opened her lips as if to say something further, then closed them again, placing them tightly together. Her eyes held a strange brightness, but he thought it was only the moon shining directly into them as they swung around a sharply-angled bend in the trail.

Half an hour later, they rode in a small bunch down the side of the pasture and into the quiet courtyard of the homestead. Dismounting, Dane turned his horse loose into the corral, closed the gate, then followed the girl inside. The rest of the men went over to the long bunkhouse.

In spite of the lateness of the hour, Dane found Maller himself, waiting for them. He was seated in a wheelchair, a heavy coat around his shoulders, but some of the old fire was back in his eyes and the colour back in his cheeks.

He glanced at Dane as they entered, then looked round at the girl. 'I see you managed to break him out of jail, daughter,' he said quietly. He nodded. 'Was there any trouble?'

'None that we couldn't handle, father,' Victoria answered. 'We had to knock out the deputy and night marshal, but apart from that, there was no trouble.'

'Good. There's been a heap of ridin' in the hills yonder. A couple of the boys came in with word of it. Seems that outlaw band are on the move again. Any idea what they could have in mind?'

Dane gave a tight-lipped smile. 'I reckon I can answer that, sir,' he said softly. 'Clem Keeler wants to make sure I don't testify against him if I'm tried. He'll be ridin' into town to be sure I don't get that chance. Either a lynch mob, or they'll attack the jail. Tonight, I felt sure that was what was happening.'

The other nodded his head slowly. 'When they find you're not in jail, they will come lookin' for you. This will be one of the first places they will come.'

'I realize that.' Dane looked over at him quickly. 'I figure it would be better for everyone concerned, if I was to ride out before sun-up and head into the hills. I don't mean to run from him. But I'd like to meet him face to face at a place of my own choosing.'

'He's a dangerous man. More dangerous than Skinner or any of the cattlemen. They were nothing more than a bunch of trained killers. They carried out orders, but they never had to think for themselves. Keeler is different. He's sly and crafty and you'll have to be good to outsmart him. One wrong move means death.'

'I've known that for a long time, ever since I rode out after him. Unless I do catch up with him, alone, I'll never be able to clear my name. Those wanted posters have been spread clear over this, and half a dozen, other states.'

'How do you figure on separatin' him from the rest of that cut-throat gang of his?'

'That sure is quite a problem,' mused Dane. It was something to which he had, in reality, been giving considerable thought, but as yet he had not come up with any solution. True, Keeler had been in town that morning and he had managed to surprise him in his role of an honest and upright citizen of El

Amaro. But the other would be on his guard now, would be doubly cautious once he learned that Dane had escaped from the jail. Whether he would consider it likely that he would dare to return to town after what had happened, knowing that he would be either shot or arrested on sight, was a different matter.

Maller eyed him closely, then smiled. 'Reckon it's somethin' you can sleep on anyway,' he said. 'You look as though you could do with a good night's sleep.'

Dane touched the bruise on his face, winced a little, then nodded gratefully. 'I guess you're right,' he nodded.

*   *   *

Stretched out on the long bed, in one of the rear rooms of the house, with the sheets cool on his aching body, Dane clasped his hands at the back of his neck and stared up at the ceiling of the room, turning things over in his mind.

The anger in him bit deep, a penetrating thing which would not be stayed and there was a coldness in him that was more than the mere chill of the night air in the room. The past few months had not been easy. Always trying to keep that one short jump ahead of a sheriff's posse, never knowing, whenever he rode into a town, if he would find his picture on one of the trees or pasted on a wooden wall, warning all of the citizens to be on the look out for him, to shoot him on sight. Then there had been the bounty hunters, cruel, hard men, killers who stayed just inside the law, men with a licence to kill, collecting the reward money for wanted men.

He recalled the look on Clem Keeler's face when he had made him stand on his feet and move out into the passage of the hotel, when the other had seen, for the first time, that he could not be protected every minute of the day, that there were unguarded moments, when he could be taken defenceless and by surprise, when the odds against him were even, and he might lose his life, challenged to draw against a man he had wronged in fair fight.

He should have shot him down then, he thought tightly, fiercely. His hands clenched themselves into hard fists with the fury of his anger. He had had his chance, but he had let it go, because he had not been the sort of man who shot down another in cold blood, without giving him an even break, a chance to go for his gun. Maybe if he had left that gun on the table in front of Keeler, maybe if he had made him go for it then, in front of the others —

He lay still on the bed as the rush of memory exhausted itself in his mind. His brain seemed empty and hollow, his body like a mere shell from which everything else had been removed, burned out. He turned his head, stared for a long moment at the floor, where the moonlight laid a pattern of light and shade on it, as it streamed into the room through the window.

Was Keeler out there now, unsleeping, making his own plans to get rid of him? Would he dare to risk his men in an attack on this place, if he should guess that he was here? It seemed unlikely. But he had underestimated Keeler once before; it was essential that he should not do the same again.

Outside, the wind made little crackling noises in the bushes near the back of the house. Reluctantly, he turned over on to his side, feeling the ache still in his chest from the brutal beating he had taken. Then everything was gone from his mind as he drifted towards sleep.

6

Trail of Revenge

Next morning, as soon as it was light, he went out into the courtyard, walked over to the corral and hitched himself up on one of the long posts. The sun was not yet up and only a greying in the eastern sky showed that a new day was on the way. Dane lit himself a cigarette, puffed on it slowly. There were a couple of men starting their chores around the bunkhouse, but beyond a glance in his direction, they paid him little attention. The air still held some of the chill of the night to it, but he paid it no heed. He was too troubled with his own thoughts to bother about that slight discomfort. Old Maller had hit the nail on the head a few hours before, when he had asked how Dane intended to get

Keeler alone. That was the only way he could possibly work it, and have a chance of a fair draw. If he bumped into the other either in town, where he had plenty of friends among the townsfolk, or out in the hills with his gunslingers at his back, there would be no chance for him at all.

But it was not going to be easy to catch Keeler on his own; not now with the other almost certainly aware that he was loose again, that the plan he and his father had concocted to get rid of him in a way that would make it look legal, had failed. But he didn't want Keeler and his men to come riding here; did not want to drag these people into his own quarrel if it could be helped.

There was a movement on the porch and a second later, Victoria came out, stood for a moment looking about her, then stepped across the courtyard to him, a faint expression of surprise on her face.

'You must have got up early,' she

said, smiling. 'How do you feel now?'

'A lot better, thanks,' Dane grinned. He nodded in the direction of the trail winding across the pasture. 'Unless I miss my guess, pretty soon, Sheriff Keeler and a posse will come riding over the hill yonder. Won't take too much for him to figure out where I've gone to earth and he won't waste any time before he comes lookin'.'

'He won't find you here,' said the girl confidently. 'You're quite safe.'

'I don't want to involve you in this,' Dane said stubbornly. 'I know Clem Keeler. I know his kind. Smooth and slick-talking on the outside, but with the characteristics of a prairie wolf behind that mask.'

The girl's expression again grew solid and resisting. 'But how do you expect to be able to fight a man like that alone, particularly with all of those men behind him? You'll need every man who can use a gun that you can get to ride with you.'

Dane shook his head, his features

hard. 'A bunch of men like that would be no good. They'd be seen the minute they rode into those hills and Keeler would know every move they made. But one man can ride other trails, can find his way across country where they won't think of lookin' and can hide where a party of men would find no shelter.'

The girl touched his arm as he sat on the rail, bringing his face round. She was smiling for him. 'At least lay low for today. If there is a posse heading this way, you don't want to be caught out there on the trail.'

He considered that, knew that what she said made sense; and nodded. After breakfast, he took his horse from the corral and rode to the top of the pasture. The sun was up, but still low on the horizon and the valley at his back still lay in shadow. From his vantage point, he could look down on the trail for several miles, to where it wound away over the next rise. It was quiet and deserted as far as the eye could see. Dismounting, he hobbled his mount and sat down on a smooth stone, feeling the quietness crowd in on him from all sides. Down below, on the slope at his back, the small herd was being moved over to the far edge of the pasture, the riders circling the rim as it moved in a solid brown mass, away from the trail. Dane forgot them almost immediately and, save for the occasional reminder of the low, deep-throated bawling of the steers, he forgot that there was anyone else around. He was nursing a very strange feeling and even the smoke did not help him materially. This mood made him feel irritable and unsatisfied, a formless feeling that would not dissolve, nor go away, no matter how hard he tried to forget it. It had come upon him at the moment when the sheriff had stepped out of the hotel lobby at his back and turned the tables on him, had been with him during his stay in that cell and had ridden with him all the way back to this place.

He sat loosely, muscles relaxed, drew smoke deeply into his lungs. In the past days, before he had met up with Clem Keeler, there had been nothing like this that he could remember. He had met every day as it came; and the feeling had been good. The past had been something forgotten and the future was, as yet, unknown. Only the present had mattered then, and riding the countless trails had been good, strong to his senses, providing him with a sense of fulfilment and contentment.

Now there was this endless running from the law, this need for vengeance on the one man who had abruptly changed all of the old ways, a need that had to be satisfied before he could feel himself again, before he could even begin to find himself once more.

He jerked his head up abruptly. Far off, at the very end of the trail, there was a faint cloud of dust. Narrowing his eyes against the sun, he tried to make out how many riders there were, but they were too far away and the sunlight was strong in his eyes. He sat quite still, tautly upright, watching them come on. They rode at a fast pace, pushing their mounts, making no effort to conceal their approach; and this alone suggested that it was a posse from town, coming out to look for him. Slowly, without haste, he whistled up his mount, tightened the cinch under the animal's belly, then swung up into the saddle and rode slowly down the trail through the pasture, his thoughts troubled, still not sure what he could do. Would Sheriff Keeler insist on searching the place? If he did, would the girl allow him to do so, or would she try to prevent him? Whichever she did, they would either run him to earth, or suspect strongly that he was there.

The girl was on the porch as he rode into the courtyard, dismounting on the fly. When she spoke to him, her voice held a certain roughness. 'What is it, Dane?'

He jerked a thumb in the direction from which he had come. 'I reckon it's the sheriff with a posse from town. They're ridin' hell for leather along the trail, making no effort to hide themselves.'

'Get inside the house. I'll deal with them,' she said firmly. She called to one of the men, motioned to him to take Dane's horse out of the courtyard and into one of the barns. It would have been far too obvious in the corral. Dane hesitated, but the girl had already caught hold of his arm, was pulling him in the direction of the house.

'You'll be safe here,' she told him. Leaving him in the parlour, she closed the door and stepped out on to the porch again.

Five minutes later, there was the thunder of hoofs in the courtyard. Pressing himself tightly against the wall beside the window, Dane glanced out, saw Keeler and a dozen or so men ride up to the front of the house and rein their mounts in a tight bunch. The sheriff eased his mount out from the rest, halted it a few feet from the house as the girl got up from her chair and walked down into the courtyard.

'Sheriff Keeler,' she said, mildly surprised. Dane picked up her words clearly through the half open window. 'You looking for somebody?'

The other touched the brim of his hat stiffly. 'Sorry to trouble you like this, Ma'am,' he said thickly, 'but we're huntin' down a bunch of men — maybe half a dozen of 'em. One or two may have been wounded. The last we heard they were headed this way. One of 'em could be that friends of yours — Dane Averill.'

Dane saw the girl lift her brows in surprise. 'Nobody has ridden through here for close on a couple of days, Sheriff,' she said quietly. 'What happened?'

'Outlaws rode into town durin' the night and busted this *hombre*, Averill, out of the jail. Always figured he was in cahoots with that bunch. Now we know for sure.' The other turned slightly in his saddle, jerked a thumb towards the men behind him. 'I got the posse out and we're aimin' to ride 'em down. Most of 'em were killed in town. We had nearly the whole bunch surrounded, but one or two got clean away, Averill among them. Could be they're clear out of the territory by now. If so, then they're beyond my jurisdiction.'

'You say the outlaws rode into El Amaro through the night?' There was genuine surprise and puzzlement in Victoria's voice now.

'That's right, Ma'am. I figured they might try somethin' like that. Had some men ready when they rode in. Reckon they didn't expect any trouble. We emptied most of their saddles before they even reached the jail.'

'Sorry I can't help you, Sheriff. If they rode through here it must have been through the night.'

Keeler considered that, then rubbed his chin thoughtfully, let his gaze wander over the bunch of horses in the corral, his keen-eyed gaze missing nothing. Finally he seemed satisfied, nodded, touched his hat again, and signalled to the men. They began to wheel out of the courtyard.

'Reckon we'll go on lookin' for a while, Ma'am,' he said as he pulled on the reins. 'But if they've got any horse sense at all, they'll head clear for the border and stay there. If any of 'em sets foot in this part of the territory they know what's comin' to 'em.' He rode off after the men, the cloud of dust lifted by the pounding hoofs settling slowly.

The girl came inside, stood in the doorway looking at Dane for a long moment without speaking. Then she said softly: 'I reckon that answers one of your questions for you. Clem Keeler must have got clear away or his father would have known and he wouldn't have been able to hide his feelings like that if his son had been killed or wounded in the gunfight.'

Dane nodded thoughtfully. This was a turn of events that he had not anticipated. The fact that the outlaw band had been busted up gave him new hope. Clem Keeler would be in town now, he decided, trying to act the part of a solid citizen of El Amaro, knowing that he had made a big gamble during the night and it had failed to come off. For once, the dice had been loaded against him, although he must not have known it when he had ordered his men into town, to kill him. It seemed ironic that it had been his own father who had smashed this band of killers.

He tried to put himself in Clem Keeler's place at that moment. He had lost everything. The men he had used to rob and plunder were killed or scattered to hell and beyond. He was alone, but what was worse, there was still one man in the territory waiting his chance to kill him.

'What will you do now?' asked the girl softly. 'Go riding after Clem Keeler?' The way she said it made it sound as if she had already made up her mind on that point and only wanted him to answer, to confirm it.

He nodded tightly. Disturbance came and unsettled her perfect assurance. She walked to the window, stood with her back to him. Her voice was small and tight as she said: 'Do you think that killing him will solve anything now. He's finished. Everything he had, evil though it was, has been smashed. He's no danger to you, or anyone else now.'

'You don't really believe that yourself,' Dane said shortly. He turned at a sudden movement in the doorway. Maller pushed his way into the room, sat in his chair, looking from one to the other, sensing what was between them.

'Who was that rode in, Victoria?' he asked. 'I thought I heard riders out there in the courtyard a little while back.'

'It was just Sheriff Keeler and a posse,' answered the girl evenly. 'They caught that outlaw bunch in town last night when they tried to attack the jail. Evidently they were wanting to break Dane out so that they could kill him.

We must have got him out ourselves just in time.'

Maller nodded his head ponderously. He seemed like a cold and distant spirit lost in thought. Dane watched the other pull himself back into the present with a conscious effort. He lifted his right hand, made a stiff, jerky movement with it. 'You know what it is you have to do,' he said, placing his powerful, keen gaze on him. 'A man has always to do what he thinks is right, otherwise he ceases to be a man. The hills are an evil place, inhabited by evil people. It may be that one of the men they took prisoner will talk. There are few men who will die for somethin' while their leader goes free and unsuspected.'

The other ceased to smile as he spoke. For a moment, his thoughts were strangely distant things. Then he pushed himself over to the window, sat in front of it, looking out.

'When I first came out here, I found only wilderness, overgrown with thorn and sage. But I saw something in this valley and I knew it was the only place for me. I went to Virginia City and bought the rights to this valley. They told me then that it wouldn't be easy to make anythin' of it. They said that it would be one thing to take this place and another thing to hold it. The ranchers wanted nothin' of the nesters, the sodbusters.' His tone grew harsh and bitter as he went on: 'I discovered what they meant soon after I came here. That was before I brought Victoria and her mother out here from back East. The first house I built here was burned down less than two months later. I appealed to the sheriff in town but he said there was nothin' he could do and that's been their attitude ever since. But if they figured they could scare me away with their threats and raids, they were mistaken. This is goin' to be a big country one day, and it will be men like me, and the others who've settled here who'll make it great.'

'But first we have to rid the country of this outlaw breed,' muttered Dane.

'Yes,' Maller said. He looked long at him, something half formed on his lips. Dane saw caution hold him back. Then he said: 'Men like Clem Keeler.'

★　★　★

The setting of El Amaro on the high break of land with the hills rising up at the back, cutting out on the skyline, made a not unattractive picture as Dane rode along the twisting trail that cut through the rocks towards the river. He had met nobody along the trail from the valley, guessed that most of the men were out riding with the sheriff, scouring the hills for a sign of the outlaws who had managed to get away. He had ridden recklessly most of the way, something that was not a normal part of him. But there was a deep and driving tension riding him now, something he could not throw off, could not ignore. There was the chance that Keeler might decide to ride out of town and head for the border to the south and if he did that and got a start on him, the chances of catching up with him before he was in Mexico were slender indeed.

Dust-streaked and dirty, he crossed the narrow wooden bridge, then swung off the trail, moving around the outskirts of the town, deliberately avoiding the main street. He entered El Amaro from the east, along one of the narrow, twisting alleys, piled high with rubbish in places. His face seemed to have been carved from granite under the wide-brimmed hat, his eyes moving restlessly under the thick brows. A couple of drifters, loafing at the end of the alley turned their faces towards him in frank curiosity, then dropped their gaze as he outstared them.

Sliding from the saddle before he reached the main street, he tethered the bay to a short hitching rail at the side of one of the buildings, eased the Colts in their holsters, then edged forward, eyes alert, stepping out on to the boardwalk with a quick glance up and down the street. There were plenty of people about, but none of them gave him a second glance as he moved in the direction of the hotel. This time, he thought grimly, he did not intend to give the clerk a chance to slip out and spread a warning. Not that the other would be able to go running to the sheriff this time, with the other more than twenty miles out along the valley trail.

The door opened under the palm of his hand and he stepped into the cool dimness of the lobby. The clerk was seated at the back of the desk, reading a newspaper and did not look up until Dane was right on top of him. Then he lifted his head, saw Dane standing over him and his mouth dropped slackly open, fear leaping into his eyes.

'Don't try anythin' funny this time,' Dane snapped. 'You got away with it once, but not again.'

The clerk licked his lips nervously, his gaze flickering from side to side as if seeking help from any direction. Dane saw his shoulders sag a little as the realization came to the other that there would be no help. 'We're still keeping your room for you, Mister Averill,' he said jerkily.

'That can wait,' Dane told him sharply. His eyes bored into the other's. 'At the moment, I want Clem Keeler. Where is he?'

'I don't know, Mister Averill. He didn't come in last night and — '

The Colt in Dane's hand clicked ominously as he thumbed back the hammer. He saw the beads of sweat that started out on the other's face, trickling down his cheeks in tiny, glistening rivulets. 'Don't push your luck too far,' Dane warned. 'I know all that happened in town last night when those outlaws came ridin' in to kill me. I know that this bunch of coyotes are finished, but Keeler is still on the loose and I guess you know where he is.'

'But I tell you that he — ' The other's head jerked back as Dane thrust the gun into his chest, reaching out with his other hand to grab the man's coat, hauling him forward over the desk. He swallowed thickly, then muttered: 'All right, if you really want to know, he came in just after sun-up this morning, went up to his room, packed a saddle roll and rode out of town.'

'Which way did he go?'

'South, I guess. Ain't likely he'd ride north after the posse.'

Dane pursed his lips tightly. That made sense, he reckoned. 'You know where he kept his horse?'

'At the livery stable, a little way along the street.' Terror showed on the clerk's face now.

Dane released his hold on the man's coat. He saw the other's shocked look, but disregarded it. Motioning the other around the desk, he forced him to move up the stairs to the top floor, to the end of the passage. The door of Keeler's room was closed, but it swung open as Dane twisted the handle. He didn't knock or even listen, but palmed the door open and cocked the hand gun.

The room was empty as the clerk had said, but there was plenty of evidence around that the other had left in a hurry. The sheets on the bed had been pulled aside and one of the pillows lay on the floor where it had been flung into the middle of the room. The drawers of the sideboard near the window hung open, some of their contents spilled on to the floor.

'There you are,' said the clerk in a high-pitched tone. 'Now maybe you'll believe me.'

Holstering his gun, Dane nodded. 'You got any keys to this room?' he asked. The other hesitated, then dug into the pocket of his coat, came up with a bunch of keys, selected one and handed it to Dane.

'Thanks.' The other grinned. 'Like I said earlier, I don't intend to give you the chance of getting men on my trail again.' Turning quickly, before the other could make a move, he stepped out of the room, swung the door shut, fitted the key into the lock and turned it quickly. The clerk pounded on the door with his fists for a moment, then stopped abruptly as Dane called out. 'Better stay where you're safe. If I see you again before I ride out of town, I'll kill you.' It was a threat he did not mean to carry out, but clearly the other had learned a lot of the rumours about this man during the past day or so and as Dane walked quickly along the passage and down the stairs, there was silence behind him. The clerk was obviously taking no chances.

Turning on his heel as he passed out of the hotel doors, he cut back into the alley, mounted up and rode along deserted back streets until he came upon the rear of the livery stable. Here, it opened out into a wired yard, filled with refuse and rubbish. Long shadows lay over the yard but there was still the heat of day on his shoulders as he slid from the saddle and walked slowly into the dim maw of the building. The liveryman was nowhere to be seen as Dane moved among the stalls, some occupied, others empty. Going into the office, he found it empty, was on the point of moving out into the street, heading for the saloon where he guessed the other might be at his dinner, when he spotted the man heading back to the stables. Dane waited in the shadows, out of sight, until the other drew level with him, then stepped out beside the man. He saw the startled expression on the other's face as he peered into the gloom, trying to make out who it was.

Then Dane saw a glint of recognition come into the man's eyes, saw the other's gaze flick away in the direction of the sunlit street, just visible through the half open doors. 'Better not try to make a run for it,' Dane said with an ominous softness to his tone. 'All I want from you is a little information, but it had better be the truth if you know what's good for you.'

'If it's anythin' to do with that darned ruckus durin' the night I don't know anythin',' grunted the other, his eyes swivelling back to Dane. He put up a hand and scratched his stubbled chin with a rasping sound which was oddly loud in the confined silence of the stables.

'I want to know when Clem Keeler picked up his horse and rode out this mornin'.'

'Clem?' There was surprise on the other's grizzled features. 'He took it out about half an hour after sun-up. Came in and left one he must've been ridin' all night by the look of the critter.'

Dane's lips parted in a faint smile. Everything was beginning to check out, but there were still some things he needed to know. 'You see which way he went?'

'Sure did. Lit out of town, headin' south, as if all the devils in hell were on his tail. Never seen Clem in such a goshdarned hurry before.'

'South,' said Dane. 'You're sure of that?'

'Course I'm sure,' muttered the other. He seemed to have regained some of his composure now, seemed convinced that the man in front of him meant him no harm. 'Struck me as funny he should head that way unless somethin' had happened. Every other time I've seen him ridin' out, he headed north. Up into the hills.'

'All right. You know what he was packin' when he left?'

The other pursed his lips in sudden concentration. 'I know he had a brand new Winchester in his saddle scabbard, and he took along a bed roll. Looked to me as though he meant to do some hard ridin' — and he'll be away quite a while.' The white brows narrowed in sudden thought. 'Say, you don't reckon he did have anything to do with them outlaws, do you?'

'Wouldn't surprise me in the least,' muttered Dane. He turned and jerked a thumb towards the rear of the stables. 'You'll find my horse back there. Bring him in and stall him until I get back. I reckon there's enough here to cover that and his grain.' He thrust a bundle of bills into the other's hand.

The liveryman stared down at them for a moment, then nodded quickly, pushed the money into the pocket of his trousers. 'Sure will, Mister. Ain't you doin' any more ridin?'

'I'll pick out one of your other horses,' Dane said. 'My own is pretty tired, been ridden all day. And I'll need a fast bronc with perhaps a streak of meanness in him.'

The other nodded in understanding, then turned and went out to the back of the stables. While he was gone, Dane moved around the stalls, examining the animals there. He finally chose a quarter horse from the last stall at the back, a tough little horse which he knew from past experience had been bred so that it was almost impossible to ride it into the ground. There would be plenty of life in it, he reckoned, enough to enable him to catch up with Keeler if he had taken that trail towards the Mexican border.

When the liveryman came back with

his own bay, he unhitched the reins and saddle, fixed them on to the quarter horse, tightened the cinch, then swung up into the saddle. For a moment, he sat there, looking down at the liveryman. Then he nodded his head slowly as he saw the gleam which came suddenly into the other's eyes.

'Better not tell anyone you've seen me,' he said tersely. 'This is just between Keeler and me.'

The man nodded. 'I get your meanin', mister,' he murmured. He drifted off into the shadows, leading the bay. Dane edged his mount forward into the main street. Digging rowels into the animal's flanks, he felt it respond fiercely, head jerking up in pain and anger. Scarcely anyone turned to give him a second glance and the houses on either side of the street fell behind him rapidly, until he was out in the open, heading south.

Would Keeler head straight for the border? Dane wondered; or was there a cache somewhere up in the hills which he intended to take with him? There would be no point in riding south into Mexico without some of his ill-gotten gains. On the other hand, if he figured that Dane was on his trail, he would waste no time in putting as much distance between him and his pursuer as possible. Thinking it over in his mind, Dane reached the conclusion that even if Keeler had backtracked for any hidden cache he might have had in the hills, he would have had ample time to swing back on to the south trail by now and the only effect such a move would have had, would be to decrease the distance between them, which would be all to his own advantage.

The hills lifted in front of him, breaking up the skyline; but to his left, there was just the open wasteland where only the bitter sage and mesquite grew, land which was useless both to the ranchers and the nesters. Maybe someday, they might make it bring forth fruit, he thought, but he did not think that would be in his lifetime.

Sitting tall in the saddle, he let his gaze swing over the country, seeking a high spot on the trail from which he might be able to look out for some distance ahead, where he might be able to catch a glimpse of dust kicked up by a fleeing man. The trail went curving away to the south in a wide ribbon, a pale grey scar on the face of the plain. It was several miles to the nearest wooded hill that lifted from the prairie but he made for it, even though it lay some way off the trail. Angling up the steep slope, he reached the top and drew rein. Far off, below him, the ground moved away, flat as far as the eye could see, until it reached the foothills of the tall peaks in the distance, perhaps a full day's ride distant.

The sunlight slanted down into his eyes, making them hurt like fire in their sockets. Dust had worked its way under the lids, grating whenever he switched his gaze from one point to another; but in spite of this, he forced himself to examine every bend and curve of the trail to the point where it vanished into the sun-hazed distance. Far off, in that desolate and broken land, he spotted the tiny black speck in the distance, spurring away from him, lifting a cloud of dust no bigger than a man's hand against the stretching landscape.

What he saw pleased him. He did not doubt for one moment that the man who was riding hell for leather along that stretch of the trail, was Clem Keeler. The other would ride until he had driven his mount into the ground. When that happened he would be forced to continue his journey on foot, or lie up and wait until his horse was rested. As for Dane, he knew that in a country as vast as this, a man had to conserve his horse, otherwise he was finished. The other would stick to the trail for as long as he could, hoping to hold the lead he had. But Dane knew better than most, that on this kind of terrain, speed was not the first essential. No horse could continue to be ridden as Keeler was riding his for long. Sooner or later, it would be finished and there were no ranches in this part of the territory where he could get himself another mount.

Putting his mount down the far slope, he regained the trail, rode along at a steady lope, letting his mount pick its own gait, knowing that it would carry him further than that which Keeler was riding. Slowly, the miles passed. From the trail, he could see no sign of Keeler, but that caused him no concern. The other would lose himself for ever if he left the trail and took to the hills on either side and Keeler, whatever else he was, was no fool; would have realized that before he had ridden into this country. His only hope now lay in getting across the Mexican frontier and losing himself in the countless villages and towns that lay within a few miles of the border.

Dane felt reasonably certain the other would stick to the trail. Heat was a dull, burning pressure on his head and shoulders and the sunlight, harsh and glaring, glinted off the metal parts of the bridle, sending painful flashes into his eyes. Around him, the burnt-brown desert stretched in endless miles to either side, with only a clump of cactus, sage or bitterroot dotting it here and there. The smell in the air that sighed over this country was compounded of baked earth, long-dried grass and the strong-bitter dust, most of it kicked up by the passage of the man in front of him.

Although impatience tended to be strong within him, he contained his feelings and contented himself with travelling steadily, rather than trying to rush things. The punishing heat lifted an invisible turbulence all about him. The lifting hills in the distance shook gently as if he were looking at them through a layer of agitated water. Halfway through the afternoon, with the sun glinting from his right, he reached the narrow river whose sandy bed was covered with less than six inches of sluggish water. Pausing to give the stud a drink, he sat on a low knoll of ground, rolled a smoke. Drawing his knees up to his chest, he stared off over the river, his features solid with purpose. The smoke burned the back of his parched throat and he gained no refreshment from it. When he had finished, he drank half of his water, then filled his water bottle at the river, corking it securely and clipping it to his saddle.

When he climbed into the saddle, he continued south. In places, the trail was almost non-existent but here and there he spotted sign of Keeler in the dust. He rode until the darkness of night came close on the heels of the brilliant red sunburst in the west. The shadows stretched themselves over the face of the desert and there was a sudden chill in the air. Shivering, he touched spurs to his mount, forced the tired animal to increase its gait for a while after darkness had fallen. He held to this gait until he reached a small hollow, a depression scooped out of the earth in long ages past. Clumps of sage and thorn grew in profusion around the rim of it and it looked the best possible place to make camp that he had seen during the whole of the afternoon and evening.

Putting the stud on picket in a small square of coarse grass, he made himself a meal, building only a small fire. He did not think it likely that Keeler, wherever the other was, could spot his fire back here, but the rim of the depression would hide it from view unless the other was already high in the foothills in the distance. Finishing his meal, he drew his blankets beyond the ring of light from the fire, pulled them up around his neck, listened to the slow movements of the horse nearby and watched the pitch blackness of night draw in over his head.

There was a small wind that rustled eerily through the brush on the edge of the hollow, making creaking sounds in the stiff branches. With an effort, he fought to still the sense of impatience that was still there at the back of his mind. Keeler would not be such a fool as to try to push his mount on through the night without a break. If he tried that, the horse would be dead under him halfway through the next morning and he would be finished. Without a mount, he would get nowhere, would be a sitting duck by the time he, Dane, came up on him.

Carefully, he reached out for his gunbelt, placed it under the blankets next to him. The flames cracked among the dry wood throwing little red sparks up into the cool night air, mingling with the stars that hung in a powdering of white against the jet velvet of the heavens. Here, in the open, beside the trail, he felt quite at home. For many years, this was how he had spent his life, riding a new trail each day, as free as the wind that blew over the wide prairies. He had camped wherever night had found him, the heavens his coverlet, the ground his bed. But that simple world had suddenly turned into one he had not known before, a world that had a hundred different sides, with facets that altered each day, with problems that had to be met and overcome. He could imagine how simple it was for a man to turn into an outlaw. A man who made one mistake and found himself hounded for it until the bitterness and the anger threw him over the razor edge, placing him beyond the law. There would be few men, he thought, who could ride on, over the hills, and put all of that behind them. Anger and bitterness were emotions which ate and tore at a man's vitals.

Rolling over on his side, he built a smoke. It helped to restrain the fierce urge to hurry, to keep on riding through the night. The knowledge that Clem Keeler, the man who had framed him for murder, was somewhere on that trail ahead of him, a man riding alone and with fear in his heart, was almost more than he could force away. Every sense in him urged him to forget about sleep, to saddle up and ride, to lessen the distance between his enemy and himself.

But that was the voice of emotion, he told himself fiercely. Commonsense told him that he had but to be patient and time would deliver Keeler into his hands. He remained awake for several hours, unable to sleep, his mind tortured by the thoughts than ran through it; questions which demanded answers that he did not know at the moment. Thus far, the trail had afforded him good riding, but just before it had become too dark for him to see properly, he had noticed that ahead of him, the ground was more broken, deep canyons and needle-sharp ridges through which the narrow trail made the only possible passage. Keeler would have found it just as difficult as it looked.

He got up and put more dry twigs and branches on to the fire. The flames leapt up anew and their crackling as the faint breeze caught them, was in his ears as he finally drifted off to sleep.

* * *

He woke before dawn and lay for a moment, staring up at the still-dark sky over his head, until memories came flooding back into his mind. Getting out of his blankets, he stretched himself, rubbed some of the grit and dust from his face and cracked lips, folded the bed roll and lashed it securely into place on the saddle. This done, he cooked a quick breakfast, while the stud cropped the salt grass, then saddled up and rode out along the trail, probing ahead into the darkness.

When the dawn brightened in the east, grey bands stretching over the horizon, he was among rocks and gullies that opened up on either side of the trail. In the dimness, he scanned the trail ahead, noticed where the prints of Keeler's horse were wandering from side to side of the trail. He felt an inward satisfaction at the sight, knowing what it meant.

Keeler, anxious to keep his lead, knowing that Dane would soon be on his trail, had pushed his mount all through the night without rest. Now the animal was so tired that its rolling gait was carrying it from one edge of the trail to the other. There was no way of telling if the animal had now actually foundered under the killer; nor how far ahead they were. More than ever, he had the feeling that the other had paused, was resting his horse, knowing that without it he was trapped.

If he had done that, then he could not be too far ahead, might even have decided to lie up in the rocks, hoping to ambush him with the Winchester he was carrying. He rode constantly, not stopping once, his gaze moving from side to side as he scanned the rocks which towered around him. Here, he thought uneasily, there were too many places where a man might hide, from where he might bushwhack another man riding the trail. The thought prickled the small hairs on the back of his neck, made him doubly cautious. Whatever happened, he must not underestimate the other. Keeler would not hesitate to turn this situation to his own advantage.

Keeler was sly and steeped in evil. He knew the ways of the outlaw better than most and the fact that he had managed to get away with it for so long in El Amaro, playing this double game, was its own testimony to his craftiness. Dane touched the butt of his gun, lips curling in a hard, cruel smile.

Half a mile further on, there were the clear marks of a man's boots beside those of the horse. His smile broadened. Keeler had done just what he had expected him to do. He had been forced to get down and walk his mount in an attempt to conserve its strength, knowing that if he continued to push it any further, he was done for. Narrowing his eyes, Dane looked up into the blood-red world of the dawn as the sun began to lift clear of the horizon, touching first the crests of the tall hills with red, then the light drifting down the slopes as the sun rose higher.

He could see no one on the trail ahead of him, but now it twisted and turned in so many dizzying spirals that he could see less than a half a mile in any one direction and for all he knew, the other might be just around the next bend. The sun came into sight as he rode through a narrow, steep-walled canyon. Sunlight dazzled him when he rode out again and he blinked his eyes several times as stabs of pain lanced into his brain. Heat and light flooded the land about him.

He drew off at another narrow creek where the water came bubbling down from the hills over smoothly-polished stones, rested his mount there for a few minutes, then resumed his way. After the first quick rise of the trail, the foothills began to break up into benches of ground, flat-topped and rocky, on which very little grew. He crossed these openly, keeping a sharp look out for any movement, watching the trail for any point where the prints wandered off it into the rocks. So long as the prints were there, he knew he had little to fear from an ambush.

Somewhere through the tall hills, there would be a pass that would lead down to the desert beyond. On the far edge of the desert lay Mexico. He stretched his memory for some information of this land, found nothing. He had never travelled this trail before. He knew the villages of Mexico well, but not in this direction. Turning a bend in the trail, he stopped abruptly, reining hard. The smell of wood smoke hung faintly in the air. He felt the sudden tightness in him, cast about him swiftly, hand reaching down for the gun at his hip. Silence hung heavy around him. Edging his horse forward, he came on the tiny hollow, a little wisp of smoke still curling into the still air.

Keeler had made camp here and had ridden out not long before. At the far edge of the hollow where it overlooked the trail, he spotted the prints of the other's mount. There was no sign of Keeler's footprints and the horse tracks seemed to be running again, which meant that Keeler had rested up sometime during the latter half of the night, had ridden on again around dawn.

He nodded to himself, looked ahead. The hills lifted high now in front of him, growing steep, crowding down on the trail where it wound ribbon-like into them. Mostly the walls or rocks were sheer and there was little chance of a man being able to climb here and lie in wait for his pursuer. Keeler would be forced to keep on riding now until he got through the hills and into the plain which lay beyond them. Along the edges of the trail, there were patches of spiny cactus and the sun was getting intolerably hot. Dust logged his throat and eyes, smeared his cracked and swollen lips until swallowing was an anguished motion. There was a sourness in his mouth that would not go away and he did not dare drink too much from his water supply. There was the chance that he might not encounter any further streams here and once the trail hit the desert, there would be only the odd water hole scattered across the alkali. He wondered whether Keeler had foreseen that danger too, or whether the other was depending on finding water soon to replenish his supplies.

He rode into the deep shadow of the hills. The sunlight never penetrated here, merely touched the crests that reared high against the blue mirror of the sky; but although the light did not filter down on to the trail at this point, the heat did and the steep sides of the hills trapped it here, unmoving throughout the whole of the day. Every breath that he took burned in his throat and lungs and it felt as if his whole chest was afire with agony. The horse was beginning to feel the pace too and moved more slowly now, its gait lop-sided. It wanted to stop, but Dane refused to slow, raked his spurs over its flanks, pushed it on, knowing that he could not be far behind the killer now, anxious to get a sight of the other.

The land became greyer, covered with a deeper layer of dust. The powder caked into a mask on his face and when he rubbed at it with the back of his hand, it seemed to tear away from his flesh, leaving it raw and painful. His eyes ached intolerably with the endless strain of peering into the bright distance and every bone in his body was weary with the strain of being so long in the saddle. Closing his eyes, he pinched the lids down together, held them there until his eyes watered and he was able to blink some of the grit and dust away.

7

Showdown!

By the time he rode out of the range of hills and into the burning hell of the desert that lay beyond, he was drooping in his saddle with fatigue. It seemed impossible that a man and horse could continue so far at this punishing pace. Yet Keeler was still somewhere ahead of him, somewhere out of sight, his tracks clearly imprinted in the dust of the trail. The middle-down sun glared fiercely at him as he rode into the open and the wind that blew now from the desert hit his face forcibly as if it had been drawn over some blazing oven before reaching him. These were the Badlands, a place where a man could ride and lose himself for an eternity, where only the coyotes and the wheeling buzzards lived. Any man who came riding into this place was either a madman or a very brave man, driven by some deep purpose, some unquenchable desire.

He lifted as high as possible in the saddle as the trail lifted over a small ridge, reined his mount and sat quite still, shading his eyes with his hand, running his swollen tongue over his parched lips, as he stared off into the red-hazed distance. Was that a speck out there a little way off to his right? His eyes began to water with the intolerable glare and his vision wavered so that he could not be sure. Blinking to rid his eyes of the tears that had formed he screwed up his eyes and tried to focus them on the distant object. The desert could produce the strangest hallucinations when a man was in his condition, could make him see things which were not there.

Sure now, he nodded to himself, leaned forward to pat his horse's neck. The killer was the best part of three miles away although the clear air of the desert made him seem undeniably closer. But he was riding very slowly now, no longer keeping a straight trail. His mount must be close to finishing point and he himself was either half asleep in the saddle, or on the point of unconsciousness. Dane slipped from the saddle, walked the horse for a few hundred yards, every step he stook a probing agony in his legs. But he knew now that there was no chance of Keeler getting away from him. All around him, there was only the stretching flatness of the desert, with no place in which to hide and the border was still a long way off, too far for Keeler to make it before retribution caught up with him.

In spite of himself, Dane grinned viciously as he plodded wearily on. The other had missed his chance back there in the rocks. If he'd had any sense at all, he would have let his mount go on, lain in wait for him, shot him in the back from ambush and taken his mount. That way, he would have been safe and it would have minimized the risk to his own skin. But it had been a symptom of his mental and physical condition that the thought had apparently never occurred to him. Keeler had worked himself into a trap of his own making. Maybe, somewhere in his weary, fuddled mind, he still reckoned he had the chance to cross the Mexican border before Dane caught up with him.

Glancing up, Dane saw the small flock of buzzards wheeling against the sky, saw them dip and sway like a pack of black cards. They knew when there was death close by, he reflected inwardly. What sort of inner sense gave them that knowledge? he wondered. Creatures who fed on death; the scavengers of the desertlands.

He climbed back stiffly into the saddle, let the stud pick its own way over the alkali. Although it was far from the zenith now, the heat head still retained its piled up noon intensity. Sweat lay on his forehead and along the muscles of his back and his shirt, caked with sweat and dust, chafed with every movement he made. The only comfort he could find was the sure knowledge that Keeler was suffering the same as he was.

Watching the other's mount rather than the man, he reckoned he would catch up with them before nightfall. If he had to track down Keeler through the night, there was the chance of being caught in an ambush, of giving the other another chance to drop him without too much risk to himself. He rowelled the stud gently, felt it respond gallantly under him, knew that this horse would go on until it dropped in the saddle.

Slowly, the distance between Keeler and himself decreased. It was clear that the other's mount was unable to go much faster, was nearly through. The sense of grim exultation rose swiftly in him. He found himself gripping the reins more tightly than was necessary. Lifting his head against the light of the sun, he glared across the intervening distance. So far, Keeler had not turned in his saddle, to look behind him, to check whether or not he was being followed. All of this heightened Dane's suspicion that the other was sleeping in his saddle, his head drooping forward on his chest, oblivious to what went on around him, letting the horse find its own trail across the desert.

The weariness, although still in his body, had been pushed into the background now and he rode with the sideways hip motion of the saddle, keeping the upper half of his body absolutely still, easing the rifle from its scabbard. The distance was still great, even for a high-powered rifle but it was not his intention to shoot the other in the back. He wanted Keeler to die and to die knowing what had killed him — and why.

The sound of the lever action of the gun was sharp and explosive in the deep stillness which clung about him. For a moment, he had the impression that it had even carried to Keeler, had penetrated his sleep-drugged brain. The other seemed to straighten appreciably in his saddle. Carefully, Dane sighted the weapon, then squeezed the trigger. The crack of the single shot crashed across the silence like the slashing snap of a knotted whip. Keeler whirled as it stung, turned his head, then leaned forward in his saddle, crouching low, He kicked furiously at the animal's sides, urging it on at a tired run. Smiling thinly, Dane watched them go, knew that it could not last. The animal was flagging with every step it took. Keeler was riding it into the ground, had done so during the night and the previous day and was now paying for his folly.

A quick glance at the sky told Dane that it still needed two or three hours to nightfall. Grimly, he continued after the fleeing rider, watched dispassionately as the other's mount began to slow, stumbled, maintained its balance and slowed to a walk, its head lowered. Keeler continued to flail with his legs, kicking at the horse's flanks, but now to no avail. He threw a hurried glance over his shoulder, realized that there was no possibility of escape now, that he had to stop and fight it out man to man. He put his mount off the trail, heading for a rough patch of ground, bordering with clumps of cactus, stony ground in this wilderness of alkali dust. Reaching there, he slid from the saddle and the horse, free of its human burden, ran on for a little way, then stopped. Dane rode forward slowly, keeping his eye on the spot where Keeler had gone to earth. He knew the other would have his carbine with him, was just waiting for him to get within range, when he would open up on him.

The grim anger rode Dane now, making him cold inside. But his mind was clear, his brain working like greased lightning. He had the other trapped, out there in the middle of the desert. He did not know how much water the other had, whether he had had the sense to take the water bottle with him when he had dismounted. The other had obviously been close to panic and he could well have overlooked that in his anxiety to get under cover before Dane picked him off with a rifle. The other's horse had strayed several yards from the rocky hollow where Keeler was holed up. The ground there was too open for the other to be able to crawl towards the horse without getting a bullet in him. Maybe be wouldn't have to wait very long before he forced the other out with thirst. Sliding from the saddle, Dane remained on the off side of the stud, flexing his arms and legs. They reacted stiffly and painfully to movement. Being so long in the saddle had cramped him and it was several minutes before he was able to move out into the treacherous alkali, keeping his head low. There was a small rise of ground to his right and he moved towards it. A rifle cracked in the distance and he saw the spurt of dust where the bullet struck. Keeler had recognized his danger and was striving to keep him at bay while he figured a way out of this predicament.

'You don't have a chance, Keeler,' he called harshly. 'I know you've got no water and there's three hours to sundown. You can't reach your horse without being shot, so you're finished.'

'Damn you, Averill,' shouted the other. 'If you think I'm finished, why not try to come out here and get me.'

'No need to do that. All I have to do is sit it out here until hunger and thirst force you out. Then I'll kill you.'

'You're bluffin', Averill.' There was a little shake to the other's voice and he didn't sound as confident as he wanted to appear. 'You won't kill me. You know that if you do, you're finished. Then you'll really have the law on your tail and my father will be leadin' 'em.'

'Do you reckon that's goin' to save you? They took some of those outlaws prisoner when they tried to raid the prison in El Amaro. You know that, don't you? And you can guess that one of 'em is goin' to talk before they're through with him.'

'They won't talk,' yelled the other harshly.

'Won't they? You figure they'll hang while you go scotfree? You're a fool if you believe that. They'll talk and somebody will listen even if your father won't. There've been too many coincidences for folk not to listen.'

'Listen, Averill,' called the other after a long silence, 'I can make it worth your while to go on riding, clear into Mexico. I've got plenty of money with me, enough even for a man like you. You wouldn't have to worry about anythin' else. So I led those outlaws. But nobody is goin' to ask you where this money came from when you're south of the border.'

'You tryin' to save your life with money, Keeler,' Dane laughed harshly, the sound carrying far among the rocks. 'No dice. I've waited too long for this moment, I've spent months trailin' you. Besides, if I wanted the money, I could take it all after I've killed you.'

Keeler swore savagely, his voice

pitched a little higher than normal. Dane listened carefully, and finally placed it to one side of the hollow where the other had gone to ground. Lifting the Winchester, he snapped a couple of quick shots at where he reckoned the other to be. He saw the dust spurt up, heard a sudden sharp yell, caught a brief movement behind the clumps of cactus. The return fire was almost immediate and he knew that he had not hit the other. Swiftly, he pulled down his head as the bullets struck the ground within inches of his prone body. The other had evidently seen the muzzle flash of the carbine and had pinpointed his exact position from that. Cursing a little under his breath, Dane slithered to one side, keeping his head and shoulders well down, holding his breath. The heat of the ground under him was a powerful thing, striking up at him even through the clothing he wore. At any moment, he expected the other to fire again, but there was only silence now and he guessed that Keeler had not spotted his move. The sun would be in the other's eyes now, blinding him.

'Listen, Averill,' Keeler's voice came from the distance. 'Just what is your interest in killin' me? So I set the law on you, but that ain't so bad. I'll get more men to follow me. I've done it once and I can do it again — and you can have the top place.'

Dane laughed thinly. 'Now you're real scared, Keeler,' he called. 'All your life you've killed men when the chances were on your side. I reckon you've never had to face up to a man in fair fight. Now that it's happened, you know that you don't stand a chance. You're lyin' back there tryin' to figure out a way of killing me without risking your own neck.'

'Dame your hide, Averill.' There was a moment of silence, then: 'But don't think you're goin' to kill me, because you ain't.'

Dane said nothing, but wriggled forward a little way. He could just make out the tops of the cactus bushes in front of him, knew that soon he would be in full view of the other and that Keeler could fire at him without exposing himself, whereas he had to lift himself up to take aim. Perspiration trickled down his forehead and ran into his eyes, half blinding him. He forced himself not to think of it, unable to wipe the sweat away for fear of giving away his position.

He lay there for a long moment, not taking his eyes off the place where Keeler lay hidden. The minutes ticked by with an agonizing slowness. At last, when it seemed that the tense silence could not last any longer, he glimpsed the slow movement, saw the barrel of a rifle appear through a clump of cactus, then the humped shape of Keeler's head and shoulders. Very carefully, he sighted his own carbine on the shape, finger tight on the trigger, and waited. Keeler lifted his head a little higher, turning it slightly, still keeping it behind the cactus, obviously looking for him.

The other was clearly puzzled and apprehensive, unsure of where his enemy lay.

Dane waited for a further second, then squeezed the trigger. The blast almost deafened him. He saw the other jerk back, then heard the wild yell which broke from Keeler's lips. 'I'm hit, Averill! You ain't goin' to shoot down a wounded man, are you?'

Dane lay quite still, made no reply. He considered himself, that his slug had found its mark, but he could not be sure, and Keeler could be bluffing, just lying there waiting for him to get up and show himself, before he opened up.

The silence lengthened. Already, the desert was a shadowed place as the sun dipped lower behind the range of hills. Soon it would be dark and that would be the time when Keeler might decide to try to run for it. He cast a quick glance about him, noticed where the ground rose a little to the right of Keeler's position and began to edge himself in that direction, taking care to make no sound. Keeler was making no noise and Dane felt the tautness grow inside him. Had his shot really hit a vital spot? Was Keeler lying in there at that moment, slowly bleeding to death? Somehow, that wasn't the picture he got. Keeler was out of sight. Dane clenched his teeth tightly in his head, debated for a moment, then laid the rifle down and crawled on without it. He was now close enough to use the Colts and they did not hinder his progress as the larger weapon did.

There was a dull ache at the back of his head which originated with the heat and the weariness that lay deep within him. He blinked his eyes, forced himself to ignore the feeling. Very carefully, he worked his way forward, spiralling around the spot where Keeler lay hidden. Deep in his mind there was the inescapable feeling that perhaps he had been a little too confident, too sure of himself, and had somehow lost the initiative. Keeler had recovered extremely quickly from his surprise at seeing him so close and his defensive position was certainly better than the open ground on which Dane found himself. He was forced to expose himself whenever he wished to open fire, whereas the other was able to remain under cover when he did so. There was a sense of burning on his knees and legs where the rough ground had torn his trousers and exposed the flesh to the abrading action of the alkali.

'You still out there, Averill?' Keeler's voice cut through the silence like the edge of a knife. His voice was shrill, but it was difficult to tell if there was any pain in it. Dane smiled grimly to himself as he remained silent. The other was worried, wanted to find out exactly where he was, had probably guessed at his intention. He lay flat on his stomach for a moment, drawing air down into his heaving lungs. A coyote in the distance lifted an eerie wail, the sound drifting down through the silence, sending a shiver along Dane's limbs.

'I meant it when I said we could make a deal.' There was a note of desperation in the other's tone now, the sound of a man beginning to break under the strain. 'The money I have on me is nothin' compared with what I can lay my hands on. It's yours if you want it. Take me back with you to El Amaro and I'll show you where the rest is. Ain't nobody wantin' it now, I reckon.'

Gently, Dane moved around the rough ground. There were little, needle-sharp rocks here, thrusting themselves up from the sand, probing and tearing his flesh. Blood began to soak into the cloth of his trousers from the cuts and the palms of his hands were bleeding too. Somehow, he forced himself to continue, edging around the hollow, up the slope which lay at the back of it. From there, he reckoned, he would be able to look down right into it, pick out Keeler easily.

The other was still shouting vague promises, interspersed with oaths, trying to get him to answer so that he could pump more shots into the desert, now lying dim in the shadows of approaching twilight. Unable to lift his head, Dane was forced to concentrate on the position of Keeler's voice, using it to orientate himself. Once, he lifted his head very cautiously, an inch at a time, but although he could make out the lip of the depression behind the screen of bushes, there was no sign of Keeler. Off to his right, he could make out the shape of Keeler's mount, standing absolutely motionless, head lowered, hind legs drawn up. It had been ridden to a standstill, would probably remain there through the night in that one spot.

Keeler let the silence drag again, then grew impatient and weary of it, and challenged: 'Why don't you show yourself, Averill. Face me as one man to another and give me that even chance you're always talkin' about? Is it because you're really yeller?' The final taunt almost brought a savage reply to Dane's lips, but he bit it down in time, forced himself to ignore it. He had almost given himself away then, playing into the other's hands.

Easing his numbed body over a mass of sharp stones and flints, he paused, looked about him, reckoned that he was now almost directly behind Keeler. He waited there, and as he waited, he thought about all of the injustice that this man had done, not only to him, but to countless other people as well, people who were not even aware of the identity of the man who had brought them so much trouble and heartbreak. Clem Keeler, the respected son of the sheriff of El Amaro, one of the most highly regarded of the town's citizens. He curled his lips in sardonic amusement. If only some of those people could see him now, could hear the things that came from his lips now that he was pleading for his life. They wouldn't think so highly of him then.

He jerked up his head, narrowed his gaze. There was a movement down below him. Narrowing his eyes, he made out the dark figure that came crawling from the rear of the depression. Keeler had obviously grown impatient of waiting for something to happen, had found some courage within him, and was crawling away from his hiding place, possibly hoping to be able to slip away in the dimness of twilight and reach his mount.

Smoothly, he pulled one of the Colts from its holster, fired at the moving shape. In the dimness, his aim was bad. He knew that he had missed the other, saw him leap back into the hollow, crouch down, looking about him wildly, his face a grey blur as he tried to make out the direction from which that solitary shot had come. Dane ignored the peril of showing himself. Pushing himself to his feet, he stepped out from the rocks and moved down the slope. A stone kicked loose by one of his feet bounced noisily down the slope and he saw Keeler turn abruptly, stare up at him in stupefied amazement for a moment, then drop the carbine in his hands to the floor of the depression, his fingers spiked as he went for the guns at his waist.

Dane waited deliberately until Keeler's weapons were clear of their holsters before he made any move. Then the guns which seemed to have come into his hands by magic spoke thunderously. Keeler got off one shot that ploughed a neat furrow in the dirt at his feet before ricocheting off into the distance with the thin, eerie wail of tortured metal. Then the killer was toppling forward, bending in the middle as if all of the starch had gone out of him, arms dropping at his sides as the guns fell soundlessly into the white alkali. Their glances held for a minute, but already, a glaze was passing over Keeler's eyes. He opened his mouth and tried to speak, lips moving soundlessly. Then he fell forward, arms outspread across the rocky lip of the hollow.

Cautiously, Dane went forward, turned the other over with the toe of his boot, still keeping the guns trained on the man. But Keeler had fought his last battle, there was no life in him now. A sudden sigh left Dane's lips as he holstered the guns and stood for a long moment, feeling the coldness of the night air on his body. Suddenly, his brain felt numb and empty, oddly hollow. He had expected to feel exultation, satisfaction, a sense of fulfilment, but curiously there was nothing like that. Keeler was dead and this was also the end of the trail as far as he, too, was concerned. Darkness had fallen when he finished burying the other's body in the soft alkali, building a cairn of stones over it to keep out the prairie-wolves and the coyotes who would come around. Moving away from the place, he whistled up the stud, fixed a lead rein to Keeler's tired mount, glanced back in the direction of the tall hills, then walked a little distance along the trail before camping out for the night. Here, in the desert, the nights were bitterly cold and he found it difficult to sleep. His body was weary, but in spite of that, sleep was a long while in coming; and even after he had fallen asleep, it seemed only a little while before he was wakened by the freezing cold that came seeping out of the ground into his limbs. Nearby, the horses were moving slowly, not nervously, but not sleeping as he had expected.

In the soft moonlight which flooded over everything, the desert seemed to glow with a strange light all its own. His legs felt stiff and swollen, but the throbbing ache in his head had gone and he forced himself to sit up, rubbing the muscles of his legs, striving to bring the circulation back into them. He really should have tried to ride through the night. It was always easier to ride in the cold than in the heat of the day when a man and a horse sweated all of the moisture out of their bodies.

Sighing, knowing that he would get no more sleep that night, he pushed himself to his feet, stood swaying for a moment as lances of pain stabbed through his legs, then steadied. He drank a little water from his canteen, but his parched, dry mouth seemed to absorb it before it had a chance to get to his throat and it did little to reduce the swelling of his lips and tongue.

The land about him looked the same in the moonlight as it did when the full glare of the noon sun lay on it. Only the paleness and the cold were different. Glancing off to his left, he could just make out the small pile of stones that marked Clem Keeler's grave. Maybe someday, something would grow there, he thought and out of evil would come forth good. He tried to go on thinking along those lines but his mind refused to obey him and after a while, he went over to his horse, threw the cinch around it and swung up stiffly into the saddle, leading Keeler's horse behind him. His water bottle was almost empty and he tried to remember the where-abouts of that last spring he had seen somewhere along the trail.

By the time the grey bars of dawn

were streaking the eastern sky, he had reached the hills and was among the towering peaks. They rolled up on either side of him, huge and unchanging, always the same no matter how man changed by reason of his contact with them. He rode on into the morning while the light grew about him. Tiredness pricked at his muscles and thirst struck at him, constricting his throat, his tongue moving rustily against his teeth. As he rode, the heat increased, a burning, oppressive pressure that brought the pain back behind his eyes. He swayed in the saddle, knew that he could not stop now, that if he was to survive, he had to find water. This was the trail of death, strewn with the bleached bones of men and animals who had tried to make it to the Mexico border wihout making proper preparations.

Time and again, he thought he saw the silver-bright gleam of water in front of him, only for it to vanish before his eyes as he rode closer. His eyes too, were almost closed by the sand that had worked under his lids, inflaming them, scouring the eyeballs every time he blinked.

It took a long time to ride out of the range of hills, far longer than it had taken on the southward journey. Tilting the water bottle to his lips, he drained the last precious drop from it, felt it wet his lips but no more. Unless he found more water within the next few hours, he was as dead as Keeler.

The thought brought a little shiver to him, but he put it away, out of his mind at once. In front of him, the trail bent and twisted in a seemingly endless series of curves and loops, moving in and out of the piled-high rocks. Surely, he should have reached the stream by now, he thought dully. He could not recall having travelled as far beyond it as this. Even the fact that his mount was now tired, was moving far more slowly than before, could not possibly account for the discrepancy.

He rode loosely in the saddle, trying

to think of anything but his desperate need for water. When his horse snickered suddenly, the sound jarring on the clinging stillness, his dull, empty mind failed to grasp the significance of it, until he glanced up and saw the sharp glitter less than a quarter of a mile in front of him. Even then he did not believe it. He had long since failed to attach any importance to anything like this. But this time, the water did not fade and vanish as he rode nearer to it and after a little while, he could even hear it bubbling over the smooth stones.

Sliding from the saddle, he staggered forward weakly, moving upstream from the horses and dropped to his knees, stretching himself out full length on the hard ground. His fingers touched the water and a blessed coolness spread into his hands and through his wrists, up into his arms. Tilting his hat far back on his head, he thrust his face forward and drank deeply of the cold water. Drinking was good. It washed away the hurt inside his mouth, cooled his burning, parched lips and throat, and filled the need in his belly. When he had finished drinking, he lay there, still in the faint shadow of the tall hill on the other side of the trail and fell asleep, knowing that whatever happened, the horses would not stray from the stream.

When he woke, the sun was almost at its zenith. His body felt numbed and bruised, but his mind was refreshed. He drank his fill once more, then topped up the water bottle, got to his feet and went over to the waiting animals. Everything looked good now. The sky was a deep blue and in front of him, the last of the tall hills dropped away and the trail moved out into the open again; the last stretch before he reached El Amaro. Riding on through the long, hot afternoon, he turned over in his mind what he could do once he got back to town. There would be Clem Keeler's death to answer for. By now, either the clerk at the hotel, or the liveryman would have talked with the sheriff, once the other had ridden back into town; and there could be a warrant out for his arrest. He doubted if even the nesters would be powerful enough to help him then.

Maybe Keeler had been right in one respect. He ought to have continued riding across the flats, until he was inside Mexico, where the law of this state could not touch him. Then he had a vision of Victoria Maller and a curious softness came over him and he knew one of the reasons why he had not taken Clem Keeler's advice.

That night, he made camp on a lonely spur of rock which overlooked the trail. He reckoned he was perhaps ten miles from El Amaro, would make it there before noon the next day. He built a fire of brushwood and branches, sat beside it, feeling the warmth in his body as he ate jerked beef and bread. Wrapping himself in his blanket, he watched the bright stars, pinpoints of brilliant light, when slowly over his head and for the first time since he had killed Keeler, he felt a strange kind of peace in him. He had done what he had set out to do and now, with most of this terrible journey behind him, he was able to think clearly about what had happened.

He slept deeply that night, did not wake until the dawn was bright and the sun was somewhere just behind the tall hills. After eating a leisurely breakfast, he mounted up, rode along the trail that now led through open country. An hour passed, and then two. So far, he had seen no one on the trail, but now, far ahead of him, he made out the bunch of riders heading in his direction. Reining up his mount, he drew back off the trail. All of his old instincts came back to him with a rush. Checking the guns in his holsters, he waited with a stolid patience for the group to come around the bend in the trail. There was only one thing this bunch of men could be, Sheriff Keeler and his posse, out after him, acting on the information he had been given by someone in town.

Tightening his lips, Dane waited until they were almost on him, knew that they were bound to see his tracks, then walked his mount out of cover on to the trail, the guns in his hands levelled on them.

'Hold it right there,' he called sharply.

There was a moment's confusion as the men fought to control their startled mounts. Dane caught a brief glimpse of the star on one man's chest, narrowed his eyes in faint surprise as he realized that Keeler was not among them. Then one of them came forward in spite of the guns he held. He lowered the Colts in stunned surprise as he saw the rich dark hair under the hat placed well back on her head and the yellow bandana holding the hair in place.

'There's nothing to worry about, Dane,' said Victoria Maller quietly. She rode her horse right up to him, laid a hand on his arm as he stared at her in silence. 'This is the Marshal from

Virginia City. We heard that you were headed this way after Clem Keeler and came out to look for you.'

'Keeler's dead,' said Dane tightly. 'It was a fair fight and I killed him, but I don't expect any of you to believe that.' He looked across at the man with the star as he spoke, his face tight.

The other gave a brief nod. 'On the contrary, I do believe you, Averill,' he said quietly, his voice deep and authoratative.

Dane turned to the girl, seeking the answers to many questions that were running through his mind. She smiled broadly, nodded. 'Two of the outlaws who were wounded talked yesterday when the marshal rode in to question them.' she explained. 'We know all about Clem Keeler leading that band of killers. We also know that he framed you for murder.'

Dane felt the air rush out of his lungs as he looked from one man to another in the bright sunlight. He saw some of the men grinning and felt all of the anger and suspicion dissolving out of his mind.

'I reckon you've been through quite a lot out there,' said the marshal after a brief pause. 'Care to tell us where Keeler's body is and then I'll send a couple of my men out to check. The rest of us can ride back into town and I'll get a doctor to take a look at those scratches of yours.'

'And what about Sheriff Keeler?' Dane asked, after he had indicated where they could find Keeler's grave beyond the hills.

'He's a broken man. He took the news pretty badly,' said the other. 'Never once suspected this about his son. Curiously, I believed him when he told me that. He was a simple man who only knew how to take orders. He fell in with Skinner and did as he was told, prevented the law from being administered to the settlers as well as to the cattlemen. But the Government are changing all of that now. It will take a little time, but they've accepted that the

321

settlers must have protection from men such as Ed Skinner and sheriffs such as Keeler, who pretend to uphold the law, but only administer it to one set of people.'

'I doubt if Sheriff Keeler will stay around in El Amaro,' said Victoria softly. 'In the meantime, I know that the job my father offered you is still open, if you'd care to take it. Unless there's any other business you still have to attend to somewhere else.'

He shook his head slowly. The sense of fulfilment which he had thought would never come, had flooded into his mind now. 'I've nothin' else to do,' he said quietly. 'I think I'd like that job.'

'Then it's settled.' said the girl warmly. Their glances crossed as he edged his mount back on to the trail and something passed between them which was invisible to all but themselves.

'This is going to be a great country soon,' said the girl quietly. 'Once the railroad comes through there'll be no holding us back. We've got everything we need here and there'll be a place for everyone — yes, even the cattlemen and their herds. Only they'll have to learn to live side by side with the rest of us and forget their animosity.'

'Do you honestly think they'll ever do that?' he asked.

She considered that for a moment, then nodded. 'I'm sure they will. Men like Skinner and Clem Keeler, who want things only for themselves will become a thing of the past, soon forgotten. There'll be towns here, railroads and highways.' The way she said it, made him feel certain that what she said was true. He kept his silence, but he was looking at her with a strange expression as they rode back along the trail. She saw it and turned momentarily away, words coming to cover her confusion. 'It takes a long time for a man to find out what is right to do and then to go out and do it in spite of everything.' The way she said it struck him more powerfully than anything else he had ever known. His fingers tensed a little around the reins, then he relaxed as he felt her smile warm on him.

THE END

We do hope that you have enjoyed reading this large print book.

Did you know that all of our titles are available for purchase?

We publish a wide range of high quality large print books including:
Romances, Mysteries, Classics
General Fiction
Non Fiction and Westerns

Special interest titles available in large print are:
The Little Oxford Dictionary
Music Book, Song Book
Hymn Book, Service Book

Also available from us courtesy of Oxford University Press:
Young Readers' Dictionary
(large print edition)
Young Readers' Thesaurus
(large print edition)

For further information or a free brochure, please contact us at:
Ulverscroft Large Print Books Ltd.,
The Green, Bradgate Road, Anstey,
Leicester, LE7 7FU, England.
Tel: (00 44) **0116 236 4325**
Fax: (00 44) **0116 234 0205**

THE CHISELLER

Tex Larrigan

Soon the paddle steamer would be on its long journey down the Missouri River to St Louis. Now, all Saul Rhymer had to do was to play the last master stroke of the evening. He looked at the mounting pile of gold and dollar bills and again at the cards in his hand. Then, looking around the table, he produced the deed to the goldmine in Montana. 'Let's play poker!' But little did he know how that journey back to St Louis would change his life so drastically.

THE ARIZONA KID

Andrew McBride

When former hired gun Calvin Taylor took the job of sheriff of Oxford County, New Mexico, it was for one reason only — to catch, or kill, the notorious Arizona Kid, and pick up the fifteen hundred dollars reward the governor had secretly offered. Taylor found himself on the trail of the infamous gang known as the Regulators, hunting down a man who'd once been his friend. The pursuit became, in every sense, a journey of death.

BULLETS IN BUZZARDS CREEK

Bret Rey

The discovery of a dead saloon girl is only the beginning of Sheriff Jeff Gilpin's problems. Fortunately, his old friend 'Doc' Holliday arrives in Buzzards Creek just as Gilpin is faced by an outlaw gang. In a dramatic shoot-out the sheriff kills their leader and Holliday's reputation scares the hell out of the others. But it isn't long before the outlaws return, when they know Holliday is not around, and Gilpin is alone against six men . . .

THE YANKEE HANGMAN

Cole Rickard

Dan Tate was given a virtually impossible task: to save the murderer Jack Williams from the condemned cell. Williams, scum that he was, held a secret that was dear to the Confederate cause. But if saving Williams would test all Dan's ingenuity, then his further mission called for immense courage and daring. His life was truly on the line and if he didn't succeed, Horace Honeywell, the Yankee Hangman would have the last word!

MISSOURI PALACE

S. J. Rodgers

When ex-lawman Jim Williams accepts the post of security officer on the *Missouri Palace* riverboat, he finds himself embroiled in a power struggle between Captain J. D. Harris and Jake Farrell, the murderous boss of Willow Flats, who will stop at nothing to add the giant sidepaddler to his fleet. Williams knows that with no one to back him up in a straight fight with Farrell's hired killers, he must hit them first and hit them hard to get out alive.